MURDER IN THE LONDON LIGHTS

A POSIE PARKER MYSTERY #10

L. B. HATHAWAY

WHITEHAVEN MAN PRESS

First published in Great Britain in 2020 by
Whitehaven Man Press

A CIP catalogue record for this book is
available from the British Library.

ISBN (e-book:) 978-1-913531-12-6
ISBN (paperback:) 978-1-913531-13-3

For my Fairy Godmothers,
Anita and Greta

Central London
(Thursday 18th
December, 1924)

One

Outside, it was below freezing, and snow had started to swirl across Regent Street and its graceful curve up to Oxford Street.

Crowds of people were hurrying around in the hot-chestnut-smoked air, lugging bags and boxes of all shapes and sizes and it all felt suitably festive.

But, Posie Parker, London's premier female detective, was well and truly ensconced inside.

Five floors up in fact, in a department store: sitting in a too-low deckchair on artfully-arranged fake sand, next to a fake paper palm-tree, in the awful hot direct blast of an electric fan heater, in a simulation of a sweltering summer. It was ludicrous really.

A line of lissom young girls, all slender bronze-painted arms and legs, were parading themselves up and down a central raised catwalk. All of them were wearing frilly bathing costumes, or gossamer-thin silk summer dresses, with large, floppy hats made of paper and straw.

Everything on display was designed for the beach, or for the promenade at Cannes, Juan-les-Pins, or St Tropez. A cruise on the Nile, maybe. Africa, if you were being really jaunty.

Not for a cold, snowy December day in London.

As the models crunched on the sand of the catwalk in their impossibly-high sandals, Posie let her gaze wander over to the huge glass windows which faced onto Regent Street, where the snow was coming down now in ever-greater sheets, and the sky was darkening outside.

'How much longer now, Dolly?' she hissed at her friend, the diminutive Countess of Cardigeon, who was sitting alongside her in the row, also in a deckchair.

But Dolly, unlike Posie, was very much in her element, and she didn't reply.

Posie sighed. She'd been using her Fashion Show programme as a paper-fan, and she now tried to de-concertina the thing, for something to do.

It read:

LIBERTY'S OF LONDON WELCOMES YOU TO THEIR FIRST CRUISE COLLECTION, PREVIEWING AT 3PM ON THE OCCASION OF THE GRAND OPENING OF THEIR NEW REGENT STREET STORE!

(STRICTLY BY INVITATION ONLY.)

Posie harrumphed. Of course this was by invitation only! This was the 'Cruise Collection', after all, designed precisely with women like her friend Dolly in mind; women who were about to leave the snowy freezing wastelands of Britain for sunnier climes abroad, and who had deep pockets to pay for the pleasure of a new winter-in-the-sun wardrobe.

In Dolly's case this was because she was being forced to take the sun for medical reasons, and was departing at the end of the month for the French Riviera. But there was no doubt that Dolly enjoyed the fashion aspect of it, all the same.

Dolly was engrossed with a specially-supplied tick-box sheet, and a small purple-and-gold pencil, and whenever she saw an outfit on the catwalk which she fancied owning, all she had to do was put a cross in the relevant box, with crosses in extra boxes for the matching hat and shoes.

A near-incessant muttering of 'Lawks! Oooh, that's for me!' and 'Coo-ee! That one's a real corker!' could be heard if one listened very closely.

'How many outfits do you really need, Dolly?' asked Posie after at least another five minutes had ticked past slowly.

She watched one girl up on the stage, gangly and thin, turning slowly in a silk kimono, the fabric the colour of a sunset. The model's proportions were extraordinary, as was her golden hair and suntan, but her face reminded Posie of the fox-faced wife of her business partner, Len Irving, at the Detective Agency: pouty, sulky, churlish, entitled. And, like Aggie Irving, this model could do with a jolly good old class in smiling.

The smell of rum and burnt sugar was heavy in the air, as lurid-coloured cocktails – a riot of oranges and reds with maraschino cherries atop each one – had been handed out, and dainty Daiquiris too, with purple-and-gold paper cocktail umbrellas for decoration.

What Posie *really* wanted was a nice strong cup of tea and maybe some buttered crumpets. Or shortbread.

An Eccles cake would do nicely.

No. A scone would be perfect.

Anything to eat, in fact. There was a good Lyons Corner House just around the corner. Her stomach growled horribly.

'Dolly? Did you hear me?'

Dolly looked over at Posie suddenly, as if rising from a deep sleep.

'Sorry, lovey? How many outfits do I need? About thirty, I reckon. But I'm done! I swear it. Oh, oh! Would you look at the sweet bit of seersucker on that? The grosgrain trim! Lawks!'

Posie's friend Dolly was a former theatre wardrobe-mistress who had – through an introduction made by Posie – married Posie's dead brother's best friend, Rufus, Earl of Cardigeon, more than three years ago.

As a result, Dolly had been thrown into English High Society and had joined the highest echelons of the British aristocracy, which had not been without its pitfalls along the way. Through it all, her sharp cockney accent had survived intact, despite hours of elocution lessons, and her beautiful petite pixie-like looks – which had drawn Rufus to her in the first place – had remained unchanged. Dolly, although now slightly better dressed, was essentially the same person she always had been.

Today, Dolly looked like a tiny white owl, her fluffy and most probably priceless white-and-silver fur coat covered in shimmery silver sequins, with a matching skull-cap worn on her cropped, bleached hair. It was very much the winter look of the moment, on the covers of magazines everywhere, impractical as you like. Dolly's version of this snow-queen look had probably cost the earth. Unlike most women up and down the land who were sporting the trend, a string of real diamonds glistened around Dolly's neck.

By contrast, Posie felt ungainly and huge, and she was actually wearing a Harris Tweed coat belonging to Richard, her husband, as all of her own would no longer do up around the middle.

She was almost four months pregnant, but she felt much heavier these last two weeks, and was being told, rather irritatingly – almost daily now, in fact – that she looked nearer six months pregnant already.

The extra load did not lend itself well to getting into, or out of, very low chairs. Like deckchairs. Indeed, Posie would have left by now, but she doubted very much she would get up from the wretched chair without help. So, she was literally stuck.

She'd been dragged along to this 'Grand Opening Day' at Liberty on Regent Street by Dolly, with promises of seeing up close the glitteringly exotic Christmas decorations from the four corners of the globe, advertised for weeks now across London. There had been promises of spectacles: free Christmas food to taste; different music on every floor; Father Christmas with a real-life reindeer on the ground floor, in a grotto which was actually the normal location of the Liberty's florist. But so far, Posie had only seen the fifth floor, and *this* show.

She was thankful she had decided to come alone with Dolly; not to bring Phyllis, her adorable little stepdaughter, who would, like any four-year-old, have been going up the walls with boredom by now.

Posie crossed her arms in resignation and looked about.

This select audience of maybe forty people were spaced widely and evenly along the catwalk, to give privacy and a sense of privilege to each viewer. It was nearly all very rich women of a certain age, in black velvets and startling hat designs which spoke of expensive, unique tastes, all of them clutching the same purple-and-gold pencils, and many with servants sat far behind them, holding bags and boxes.

No-one else was in a scratchy tweed coat. Or in a fashionable fluffy white owl costume. A couple of bored husbands were here too.

On the other side of the catwalk sat an unaccompanied middle-aged man with a spreading stomach, wearing a too-loud pin-striped suit of navy and white, with a huge gold fob watch on display. He was smoking a fat cigar, and while he occasionally ticked at his little list in front of him, he seemed less interested in the show than in observing his neighbours. Specifically, the man next to him.

This next man was wearing a pearl-grey homburg hat, obviously very expensive, pulled very far down over his eyes. He wore a grey muffler too, and a matching thick, grey sheepskin coat.

He must be boiling, thought Posie. *Maybe he's all ready for a quick getaway? Or maybe he hadn't anticipated the fake heat blowing through the place like a hot storm?*

The way he had crossed his arms over his chest made Posie think the grey-hatted man was enjoying this spectacle even less than she was. She could have sworn the man was looking in her direction, but the shadow of his head coverings was too much for her to even catch his eye and share a raise of a mutually-sympathetic eyebrow. Posie looked further down along the row.

The woman beside the grey-hatted man sat engrossed, an order-list in her hand. She was simply stunning; a creature dropped from heaven. Wide-set china-blue eyes, a bob of sleek black hair, a perfect scarlet Cupid's bow of a lipsticked mouth. The clothes were something else, too: bright purple and pink velvets made up a fabulous frock with a strange medieval-Templar cross symbol embroidered in gold all over it.

Foreign, obviously. Russian? American?

Posie was just trying to get a better view when suddenly it was all finishing up, and Dolly, together with one of the purple-and-gold-suited waiters was dragging her up.

Posie took Dolly's arm and they started to walk down the vast, sweeping, curling wooden staircase, passing the crowded floors which were really galleries, all circling around and around, in rising levels, above one vast central atrium below. The entire roof was created with panels of glass which kept the place light, but it was the dark wood of the store which was Liberty's distinguishing feature.

There were dark oak beams, and floorboards, and doors and fireplaces, all merging beautifully, but that was hardly surprising, for the whole store had been famously created from the remnants of two ancient battleships.

The store was all a trick: made to look as if it were five hundred years old but really it had been built within the last two years.

The best of British tradition, but with a very modern twist.

'Do you like the shop, Dolly?' asked Posie with interest, noting the beautiful fabric department which took up two complete long galleries, and then the shoe department, and the section with baby linen on the next gallery down.

Posie explained where the wood had come from. 'I'm pleased I've seen it for real, having read all those newspaper advertisements. It's certainly very special.'

'Special?'

Dolly was lighting up one of her black-and-silver Sobranie cigarettes.

'Warships? What's so special about *that*, lovey? I just think it looks *old*. Reminds me of Rufus' old family castle up in Yorkshire.'

Dolly shivered melodramatically. 'Nah, I only came here for that little bit of summer sunshine upstairs! And they *do* seem very efficient. I gave them my leavin' date, just after the New Year, and they've promised they'll get me the lot – well, not *quite* the entire collection – by Christmas Eve. All packed and ready to travel with. That's service for you, eh, lovey! Oh, is that another cocktail? Well, no: don't mind if I do…'

Dolly helped herself to another Daiquiri, proffered on a silver tray by a boy on the next landing.

Thinking of her cup of tea, Posie continued on downstairs and reached the ground floor, the main central atrium, getting separated from Dolly in a crowd of shoppers. Posie was busy looking at the Christmas lights which hung in bell shapes in long strings from the roof, which had a dizzying effect if you craned your neck and looked up.

She smiled at the decorations which were festooned everywhere: holly and ivy, and little snippets of tinsel garlanded about the banisters with pine branches stuck about the place for good measure. The scent of the pine branches and of cinnamon and mince pies drifted over the place deliciously. If you wanted festive cheer, and could afford it, this was obviously the place to be.

Mince pies.

Posie looked about for the source of the scent.

She spied a smart young waiter behind a Christmas tree holding mulled wine and a plate of doll-sized miniscule mince pies, and before she could blink, Posie found herself being rather unladylike and grabbing up a handful. She located a handy spot against the oak-panelled wall, suitably out of the way and decorated all over with bunches of spruce. There was actually a well-hidden telephone booth here, too, also hidden by the spruce.

She was just cramming a few pies in her mouth, all in one go, and starting to appreciate the size of the queue of fractious, impatient children wanting to visit Father Christmas in his florist-perfect grotto, when she felt a gentle tap on her shoulder.

She swallowed hastily. 'Oh, hello?'

'Say, it's Miss Parker, ain't it? Miss Posie Parker?'

She turned and found herself looking up at the grey-hatted man who had been sitting across from her at the catwalk. Up close he was tall and stocky, although he carried himself with a dancer's grace.

'Do I know you, sir?'

For a second – two seconds at most – the man flipped up the brim of his grey homburg hat with grey-gloved hands, allowing the artificial lights of the atrium to play over his handsome, very tanned face.

Posie caught a glimpse of beautiful, almond-shaped, almost Arabian eyes. Eyes which made the hearts of millions of women all over the world beat a shade faster than they should.

Posie gasped. 'Oh, golly. I say! I *do* know you!'

For, unless she was much mistaken, she found herself looking straight into the eyes of Rudolph Valentino.

The most famous movie star in the entire world. An American movie star.

The Sheik.

Unless she was seeing things?

Truth be told, Posie was not much of a movie-goer, unlike Dolly, who lapped up most things at the cinema eagerly, good or bad. But Posie had in fact seen *The Sheik*, at the Marble Arch Pavilion, what seemed like years ago now.

That movie had made Valentino's name, establishing his face as perhaps the most famous of any movie star to have ever lived. The resemblance here was too similar, too much. Her heart pounded and she felt a little giddy. Posie leant against the wall. He held her arm gently.

'Is it really you? I saw you in *The Sheik…*'

A slight throaty laugh. 'Yes. Yes, it's me, Miss. I'm not the actual Sheik, though. Hopefully those days are long gone.'

But what on earth was the most gorgeous man on the planet doing standing in Liberty on Regent Street this Thursday afternoon?

'Say, Miss Parker, can we speak?'

He didn't take his grey-Napa-leather-gloved hand from her arm; kept it there, casually.

'Of course we can speak, only, how on earth do you know who I am, sir?'

Was this some crazy dream? And in the swirling hordes of people all around – children, shoppers, supervisors and sales assistants – it seemed to Posie that she and this beautiful man had formed an island all of their own, and that all the crowds around them were just an extra layer of madness.

On a turn in the staircase above, Posie saw the sulky blonde fox-faced model walking quickly down the steps with the huge man in the loud pin-striped suit, still smoking a cigar, the two linked at the elbow, mock-formally.

A father, maybe? A Manager, more like. *Yes, that was*

it. Because in her hand the model was holding onto some papers and passing them across to the man, as if they were important. Booking sheets for other fashion shows, most probably, or pay slips.

And then, suddenly in all this craziness, Posie spotted Dolly, ethereal in her white fur and sparkling jewels. In a few seconds Dolly would step onto the floor of shoppers.

Somehow the wall with its decoration of winter spruce managed to hide Posie and Valentino. They had a minute, maximum. Because Posie realised this man needed her help; was in some kind of a pickle.

'I was told to look out for you by Martin Poulson; he said you'd be here today.'

That name rang a bell.

Posie frowned. *Martin Poulson. Who the deuce was he?* She remembered suddenly. But the connection was surreal. Out of place.

'Oh? A Director at the Café de Paris?'

'That's about right. Great fella.'

The Café de Paris was a new hot-spot in town, not far from here, near Piccadilly. Arguably *the* hot-spot in town, with the best musical acts and dancing London could offer.

The place ran from afternoon tea through to dinners and all-night cabarets. There were huge queues to get in, especially on the nights the Prince of Wales – England's most dashing young bachelor – went there for the dancing. Posie had never been. Never *thought* about going. Certainly not now, looking and feeling exactly like a beached whale.

She shook her head, confused. 'I don't know Mr Poulson, not at all. But my husband, Richard, he's the Chief Commissioner of New Scotland Yard, works with him occasionally. He seems a very helpful chap.'

Mr Poulson had been head Waiter at London's famous Embassy Club, and had been taken on at the Café de Paris as one of its Directors simply because he knew everyone who was anyone in town. A subtle, ultra-polite, clever, kind man, he was known to have the ear of the Prince of Wales himself. Richard Lovelace spoke well of Poulson, of his discretion and clear-thinking manner. Poulson had helped 'locate' a couple of well-known persons at various times for the Yard, doing so in a courteous and unruffled manner.

'Poulson recommended that I speak to you, Miss Parker.'

Valentino smiled, and Posie saw with a start of surprise that there was an unmistakeable sadness in the smile. The movie star flicked his head quickly in the direction of Dolly, trapped in the crowd.

'Your pal there, the tiny Countess, was at the Café de Paris last night, dancing in all her white feathers. *Mamma Mia*! Quite some sight, ah! We were there incognito. We're here on a flying visit. Very brief. We only arrived in England yesterday evening, see? We landed at Croydon Aerodrome and hot-footed it along to the club. Your pal, the Countess, had told Poulson last night that you would be attending this little fashion show today, together. And so that's how Poulson knew where to find you; said you were the person to speak to. He knew I had this little trouble, see? I spoke to him about it at lunchtime today when I went back to the club. His recommendation worked out well: we were scheduled to come here anyway; my wife wanted to purchase the famous Liberty fabrics, see? And then she thought she'd order the entire Cruise Collection, upstairs, too, ah!'

Posie was trying to stay focused on the facts, what Rudolph Valentino was telling her. But it was difficult, because when he spoke it was completely mesmerising: his words falling heavy and slow in a not-quite-American accent; the Italian intonation of his words and the way he added 'ah!' at the end of his sentences intriguing. His voice was beautiful, low and sultry. A shame there was no way his voice could ever be heard in the movies…

But then Posie focused, grabbing onto something Valentino had said. *He knew I had this little trouble.*

'You wanted to see me, sir? *Me*, especially?' She swallowed nervously. 'Not my husband, the Chief of Police?'

'No. This is too delicate a matter, Miss. You see, ah?'

No, she didn't see at all. But she found herself nodding along like a love-struck girl.

Valentino leant in closer, his hand still on Richard's scratchy old tweed coat. Close up he smelt expensive: leather and cigar smoke and a strong, intense minty-ness mingling with the pine around.

'I can't talk, Miss Parker. Not here. We might be overheard. I've got to keep my identity a full-on secret, see? Until later tonight, anyhow.'

Posie was intrigued. 'Why are you undercover? Is it just for convenience, because you don't want to be overwhelmed by adoring fans? Or for some other reason?'

Valentino grinned. He was fishing for a cigarette case, and a lighter.

'Both. I hate being mobbed, particularly since that darned movie, *The Sheik.*'

The man cursed under his breath. '*Mamma Mia!* How I hate that film. But there *is* another reason I'm undercover until tonight. Did you see those sweet little angels hanging above the streets here? In cute little itty-bitty garlands of electric bulbs? Pretty, ain't they? Well, I've been asked by the Lord Mayor of London if I will do the honours and turn them on – the electric Christmas angels of Regent Street – this evening. They wanted a movie star and I almost literally happened to be passing. It's lucky, we're only here until tomorrow evening. But I need to keep my identity a secret until tonight at least, ah!'

'How lovely!' exclaimed Posie, meaning it. 'What a treat for Londoners to see you, and what a surprise! This is the first year they've hung electric Christmas lights in the main shopping area, and I can't think of a more suitable person to set them ablaze!'

After all, the man had set ablaze almost all the female hearts of the nation already.

'Say, you're welcome to come along with me and my gang, if you like, Miss Parker? It's at six o'clock. By that cute little Eros statue on Piccadilly Circus. It will be some event, I reckon. If it goes to plan…'

'That's so very kind. I so wish I had brought Phyllis along, after all!'

It would, Posie thought, have been something the little girl would have remembered for the rest of her life.

'Phyllis?'

'Phyllis is my little step-daughter. She's four.'

'Ah,' he smiled quickly, easily. 'How lucky you are! Yes, a real shame.'

But Posie's thoughts were racing now.

If it goes to plan…

I had this little trouble…

Behind them the tall, sulky-faced model was counting out pennies from a cheap coin-purse for the telephone booth, on her own now, swinging open the door roughly, almost hitting it into Posie's back.

'But you wanted to tell me something, Mr Valentino? You're worried?' Posie saw how he was playing nervously with the cigarette, obviously desperate to light up. 'Shall we step outside?'

Valentino checked his watch, a huge fat gold fob of a thing. He shook his head slightly. 'Three-thirty, right now. I have a driver sittin' out front, Miss Parker. You wanna take the car? I'll meet you there.'

'Where? Eros?'

'No. Back at the Café de Paris. Coventry Street. I feel at home there and you sure look like you could do with some refreshment, ah! Those tiny little pies not helping you one bit!'

He smiled that sad smile again. 'A baby on the way, Miss Parker! How lucky you are! You need to eat. For sure.

Mangia, as we used to say in the old country. And when we get to the Café de Paris I'll tell you everything. I need you to assess something for me. Meet some folks. Say, you have a spare hour?'

'Well, yes I do, as it happens. But I don't need your car; it's barely ten minutes' walk from here to Coventry Street.'

'You crazy? The snow! Widd-a your baby! No, Miss Parker. You take the car. It's a red Daimler and the driver is Frederick, both on loan from The Ritz. I will meet you at the café in about twenty minutes. Ask for Mr Poulson if I'm not yet there. He'll look after you nicely. I have to do something first for my wife!' He was lighting up, inhaling deeply.

And here was Dolly, breaking through the crowds, elbows out on either side, huge kohled eyes scanning the room.

'That all sounds fine. Shall I bring Dolly?' Posie asked quickly, seeing the man turn to leave.

He shrugged, smiled. 'As you like, ah! She sure knows her way around that place so she could always go off and chat to someone…'

'I understand.'

And then Valentino cursed silently, staring beyond Posie's shoulder. He groaned, just perceptibly. 'My wife. *That* is my Natacha. We're supposed to be doing this in a very subtle way, undercover. And here she is making a complete drama out of everything.'

Posie stared behind her to where a woman of about her own height – but at least ten years younger – was barging her way through the crowds. There was entitlement in her every move.

Posie immediately recognised her as the beautiful magenta-clad woman who had sat at Valentino's side upstairs. But now she was wearing what was obviously a crazily-expensive black fur coat with a glittering jet-encrusted cloche hat. Swathes of wine-coloured velvet scarves fluttered around her neck.

Behind this woman were several shop staff, all bearing boxes and bags, and behind them were two young lads manoeuvring an entire shop rail on wheels between them: the metal bars were packed completely with outfits; each one encased in a protective purple cladding of tissue paper. The woman – Natacha – was hollering at the young men in a disgruntled, slightly despairing voice, and her beautiful American accent seemed to ring out through the vast hall, causing many shoppers to turn and stare, their jaws collectively dropping at the extravagance on show.

Natacha saw Valentino and gave him a flicking, move-out-of-here-right-now sort of gesture, and he turned and fled, like a rabbit in a particularly strong set of headlamps. Posie almost joined the ranks of jaw-droppers, but was now completely absorbed by the attentions of her friend, who was beside her.

'You still want us to go to that dingy old Lyons Corner House for tea, lovey?' Dolly asked, fastening her coat together at the top.

Posie grinned. 'No. Actually I have a red Daimler waiting for me outside. It's going to take us somewhere I've never been before.'

Dolly looked completely confused, foxed. 'You didn't have one of them drinks too, did you, lovey? What you talkin' about? Next you'll be tellin' me you've been speakin' to Rudolph Valentino. D'you know, comin' down those stairs, for one second I could 'ave sworn I saw him! But what would he be doin' here, right?'

She took Posie's arm as they headed for the red car in the snow.

'Must be all those blimmin' Daiquiris!'

* * * *

Two

They had arrived at the Café de Paris.

Music was tinkling, ladies were laughing, and the glamour factor was high.

Their table was right next to the stage, and obviously it was the best in the place, tucked back, with a fine view out over the entire club and the stage, yet in the darkness of the overhang of the balcony above, to afford the sitters' privacy.

Posie felt herself rather crazily, and unusually, excited, as she was led by a waiter to the table, having been divested of Richard's coat upstairs. She wasn't disgracing herself too much, after all: under the coat she was wearing a beautiful dark-pink velvet devoré swing dress with matching flat Mary-Janes and a wide flat headband of pink lace. She also wore her usual string of pale pink Murano glass beads at her throat: a memory of a friend who was now long gone; a reminder of routes not taken, never to be explored.

Dolly, squawking behind her, was astonished that her friend had brought her here.

'Didn't you say we were comin' to somewhere we'd *never* been before? I was 'ere last night, darlin'! Makin' the most of town before everythin' closes up for Christmas and I get sent to France for what feels like a blimmin' prison sentence.'

'I said we were coming somewhere *I* had never been before. But I think this visit, today, will be equally unforgettable for you, too, Dolly.'

They'd obviously been anticipated, and Posie was impressed. The club was a sleek operation; despite the fact the place was very busy.

The table was laid for seven for a proper afternoon tea, with beautiful white linen and tall rising porcelain towers filled with all manner of delicious treats: cucumber and salmon-paste sandwiches, lemon-curd tartlets, mince pies with brandy butter in a pot nearby, and scones, the heat still rising from them. Tea, three kinds, was on the table already.

'Oh, how utterly perfect,' exclaimed Posie as she sank down into one of the black velvet-backed chairs, Dolly sitting down beside her, but with a bit of an ill grace. Dolly was skittish and madly excitable, eyes huge and glittery with the effect of all the cocktails.

Posie was taking it all in: the basement club with its huge black pool of a dance floor, currently set out with small round tables for afternoon tea, black-liveried waiters smoothly sailing about like gliding swans with tea-trolleys; the famous bronze gilded double staircase leading up from the club floor to a small landing above, which was being used by a band in full swing. There was another staircase rising up again from where the band played to the front entrance of the club at street level.

There were mirror-balls and fitted mirrors at every turn, with a huge, grand chandelier blazing in the very centre of the room. The sleek ebony-and-chrome art deco look of the place was given an extra dash of decoration at present, with mistletoe hung discreetly from the mirror-balls, and a small holly-and-ivy wreath placed tastefully on every table.

Posie's awed and delighted reverie was broken into by a smooth, gentle voice behind her. 'I do hope you have everything you need, Miss Parker?'

A man in his late forties, slightly rotund at the waist and with the appearance of a grizzled but friendly badger, was at her side, pouring out the China tea and adding sugar to her cup without being asked; deftly placing scones onto Posie's plate, adding cream, jam and butter in liberal quantities.

'I am Mr Poulson, and I must confess I was expecting you, Miss. I hope this is all in order?'

'Oh, quite. It's lovely. You know my husband, I believe?'

A slight nod, a blink of bright blue Scandinavian eyes, a slight ruffle of that badgery moustache. Nothing given away, no alliances or pacts admitted to unless with real reason.

Poulson poured tea for Dolly, whom he addressed formally as 'Lady Cardigeon' throughout, and Posie saw with surprise that Poulson had added a good deal of sugar to Dolly's extra-strong cup of tea, and Dolly was glugging it down without even thinking about it, not protesting one bit.

It was exactly what she needed.

So great was this man's professionalism that he'd placed a new packet of black Sobranie cigarettes at the side of Dolly's plate, but had sensibly avoided putting out any alcohol for her. It was obvious to anyone that Dolly had had quite enough already.

Dolly couldn't seem to sit still. It was as if she were fearful of missing out on the action elsewhere in the club, like a child in a sweetshop, being forced to sit and wait. Up on the stage two jazz musicians were preparing their set, and Dolly looked from them back across the big room, where a finely-built young man in full black tie, with black waxed-back hair and rather protruding ears, was weaving his way through the tables, carrying a clarinet and a conductor's cane, heading towards the stage. Once there he started to talk to the two musicians, tapping at his watch and making 'hurry-up' actions.

'Wotcha!' said Dolly excitedly. 'That's Harry Roy, the bandleader of The Lyricals, that little band who've been playing up there on the balcony. What that man can't play! And he's so young, and so gifted, and lawks, I must 'ave a word wiv 'im. You not seen him in *Photoplay Magazine*, Posie lovey? I'm goin' up to introduce myself properly! You want to come, too?'

'Oh, no. You carry on.'

Posie was aware of Mr Poulson lingering as Dolly skittered off. She desperately wanted to eat something, but felt rude starting without the famous man who had invited her here.

The Director of the club sat down briefly next to her, speaking in an undertone: 'Do start, Miss Parker. Mr Valentino would not want you to wait on his behalf. I believe he is very courteous like that.'

Posie nodded and picked up a scone. 'You know him well, Mr Poulson?'

The man smiled. 'Not at all, Miss. He came here only for the first time last night and I made his acquaintance then. We got along well, and I do believe he found this place to his liking; if there were rooms here I fancy he would have taken them. There is, after all, something of the American spirit at play here, I think. We certainly have all the popular American acts. Best of the best.'

He indicated to the stage with obvious pride. 'Mr Layton and Mr Johnstone here are New York's finest; and a favourite of the Prince himself. You're lucky to catch them on now. Normally they only play at night. But tonight, we have another American treat in store. Something which will have the whole of London talking about it by tomorrow morning.'

'Golly, that sounds intriguing. I wish I could come, but...' She indicated towards her belly, laughing. 'Quiet nights in for me, now.'

'I wouldn't worry, Miss Parker. Your friend the

Countess will no doubt be able to report on it all. In her own inimitable way.'

Posie crammed more scone in her mouth hungrily. She was scanning the staircase, which had a double 'V' leading upwards. Still no sign of the movie star. She sensed Poulson was about to leave.

'Can I ask you something, Mr Poulson? Mr Valentino suggested some "trouble", and you kindly suggested me to him, as someone who could help. But, given his famous status, sir, perhaps my husband might be a better option? If it's *protection* of some kind he's after.'

Poulson smiled enigmatically, rising. 'I think you'll find this is the sort of matter in which a woman's touch is by far the best thing. A subtle thing.'

'I see.' Although she didn't, not at all.

And while she was still scanning the room and its majestic staircase, she sensed a slight movement behind her: Poulson was suddenly drawing out chairs; a bottle of single-malt whisky appeared on the table as if by magic; ice was laid out, with a siphon of soda.

'Good afternoon, Mr Valentino.' Poulson bowed slightly, and then busied himself cutting and lighting a cigar, as Rudolph Valentino sat down next to Posie.

'Say, Miss Parker, thank you for waiting for me.'

And to Poulson: 'Much obliged to you, Martin. And for the use of that handy little old secret entrance on Rupert Street there, ah! No-one spotted us, I'm pretty darn well sure of it.'

'Very good, sir. I'll leave you. If you need anything, just wave. And, Miss Parker? I think you will find that the Countess is now with our costume designer from our extensive wardrobe department, the lovely Miss Dolly Tree. Likely as not the Countess will be with Miss Tree for some time. Two ladies who share a name, and many interests beside, I'll warrant. Birds of a feather. Now, if you will excuse me…'

As Valentino took the cigar and inhaled, Posie saw Dolly perched upon the small stage, smoking with a crazily exaggerated long black cigarette holder – surely something from the wardrobe department here? – laughing.

The ridiculous prop obviously belonged to the very young, very stocky girl at her side, whose youth was surpassed by Dolly Cardigeon's elfin beauty, but whose strong personality, expressed through a daringly low-cut, not-for-the-fainthearted jumpsuit, emanated off her in big, bold waves. Dolly Tree was no doubt a girl who, despite being very young, fitted right in here.

Valentino followed Posie's gaze and smiled in Dolly's direction. 'What Poulson means is that you and I have a little time to talk.'

He still wore his grey homburg hat, but he'd removed the muffler and his thick coat to reveal a three-piece suit, a bright blue, which, even in this overhang, looked fantastically modern; simply wonderful, in fact.

She tried not to stare too much, but she saw now how very young Valentino was.

He must be younger than me, by a couple of years at least, she thought to herself in surprise. Younger by at least a decade than Richard Lovelace, her husband.

Up this close Posie saw the bags and tight grey lines under the film star's almond-shaped eyes, and the beginnings of weary lines at the sides of that famous, sensual mouth which has kissed Agnes Ayres in *The Sheik* to the delight and simultaneous envy of women across the world.

But the tiredness and the layer of creamy make-up he was wearing, even now – for it was definitely thick orange make-up – could not detract from the absolute beauty of the man. No wonder he photographed so well.

'Are we being joined by anyone else?' Posie asked, for she was aware of the table set for seven, and the sudden arrival of a group of mostly black-clad people who were standing talking – or rather, *arguing* – next to their table, proprietorially near, but up against the wall in the convenient darkness. Were these the 'folks' Valentino wished her to meet?

'Sure we'll be joined,' Valentino motioned in the direction of the group by the wall, 'in a few minutes. See, there's Natacha, my wife? And next to her is Reed Amory, my Personal Secretary, and then the big fella next to him is Donald Derekson, my Manager from the film company I'm signed to, Ariad Films. And then there's Nita – you know her? The film star Nita Naldi? – we're great pals, of old. They'll all join us shortly. Something trivial is going on between them, nothing big. It's a helluva thing travelling with them all, forever arguing, ah! A circus, really. I just shut my ears and keep on goin'.'

Posie couldn't make out much of anyone he'd pointed to in the velvety blackness, but she didn't say so and just kept on drinking her tea, took another scone.

What on earth was this special woman's touch which was needed here?

It seemed to her that by having the famous film star Nita Naldi and a wife in tow to boot, Rudolph Valentino had quite enough of a woman's touch already.

Probably too much.

She watched with interest as Valentino took out a large expensive leather wallet, more like a document folder really, from inside his jacket pocket. He put it on the snow-white tablecloth in front of him and started leafing through, frowning and talking and smoking as he did so.

'You know why we're *actually* over here, Miss Parker? I didn't tell you before, ah! It's a funny old business, ours. Nita Naldi here and I, we've just wrapped up a big film over in Hollywood, but Natacha has written the film of her life – it's her pet project – and Nita and I committed to be the two leads. For our sins! Ariad have allowed us to come across to the Continent and buy pretty much everything – costumes, scenery, stage-sets – we need for Natacha's little film. It's gonna be called *The Hooded Falcon*, and it sure looks like being an opulent picture! We've been over in Paris, and we've stripped that city's theatres bare of all their specialist costumes and props! They sure have some fancy old stuff, ah! And we arrived here yesterday, all top-secret, and, as you saw, Natacha's already been busily buying up all of the fabrics and costumes that your sweet little city has got to offer. Perhaps old Derekson is laying into her about cutting down on the spending now, ah! It's an expensive trip for him, that's for sure. I'm sure glad it's not my money we're ripping through!'

'So your turning on the Christmas lights in London is a sort of happy accident then, is it? Not the *reason* for your visit?'

Valentino shook his head. 'Amory, my Personal Secretary, was approached right at the start of this week by your Mayor of London, Sir Alfred Bower. Amory was busy booking up hotels over here, and organising out-of-hours secret visits to places, and he had to get the Mayor's consent for a few things: a night-time tour of the National Gallery, and a private tour of the British Museum and that swell little St Paul's Cathedral. The Mayor agreed to all of Amory's requests, but he asked this one favour in return. Said he thought I'd add a certain something to the event!'

Valentino shrugged easily. 'To be honest, it's fine. It's less than fifteen minutes of my time. A little bit of well-managed mobbing is good for the soul. As long as it *is* well-managed.'

'And will this be?'

'I hope so. Apparently one of the top-dogs in your country's police force is on the case.'

Posie was intrigued. Could it be that Richard had known all week about Valentino's surprise appearance to turn on the Christmas lights? How bizarre if so! They often had to keep secrets from each other in their mutual lines of work, but it would be funny if an odd symmetry was at play here today.

'The police fella should be joining us here soon, I hope. Amory organised it all, with Donald of course.'

Now this would be odd!

Posie watched, intrigued, as the man at her side came to a stop with the documents in his wallet.

He'd been flicking through a thick wodge of carefully-cut-out newspaper clippings, with a good deal of annotation and rings and arrows in red ink. She saw the words '*REALLY?*' and then '*IDIOTA!*' several times.

Valentino looked up at her, caught her eye, shrugged, smiled very slightly, but sadly. 'I know, Miss Parker. I am very vain, ah! I insist on reading all of the reviews of my work, and then I cannot handle what I read! I get upset. It is a kind of slow torture to me.'

He looked down quickly. 'But *here*. This is what I wanted to show you, ah!'

'The "trouble"? The thing you needed me to "assess"?'

A nod, just discernible. The tanned hands with their long fingers and perfectly-buffed pink nails pulled at a card, a cheap white printed postcard such as you could buy in a pack of ten on any London news-stand, or at a cheap bookshop. This one had newsprint stuck to it. A mixture of fonts and sizes, forming individual words. The effect was at once both horrible and taxing on the eye.

'Nice, ain't it? Here you go.'

Posie read quickly:

MR VALENTINO.

YOU THINK YOU'RE SO SMART LIGHTING UP THOSE CHRISTMAS ANGELS IN A BLAZE OF ELECTRIC GLORY, DON'T YOU? AND FRITTERING MONEY AWAY ON A FUTURE PILE OF TRASH?

NOW NATACHA VALENTINO WILL BE CAUGHT IN A BLAZE.

TAKE THIS NOTE AS A WARNING: LEAVE NOW.

OTHERWISE THE GIRL GETS IT.

Then Valentino placed another note, an identical white postcard with the same mix of newspaper print cut-out letters, in front of Posie, who had to stop herself from gasping in horror.

IT WILL BE MURDER IN THE LONDON LIGHTS.

'The first was under my door at The Ritz very early this morning,' Valentino said calmly.

He poured himself two fingers' worth of whisky and started to drink it neat.

'And the second was at the Reception as I left The Ritz today. I was on my way here, actually, for an early lunch. Both came sealed. Both in white envelopes.'

He drained the glass quickly and looked into Posie's eyes, which she knew were registering her shock, although she was doing her best to appear unruffled. Posie coughed delicately, but her heart was pounding in her chest.

'I honestly think you should tell the police at New Scotland Yard. This looks to be serious. Some crazy person has managed to intercept your undercover plans. This is serious!'

She looked at her watch. It was a quarter-past four now.

'You're due to turn on those Christmas lights in less than two hours, sir! You need to speak to someone who is placed to deal with this properly. Not me. I'm a Private

Detective, not an armed guard. It sounds as if your wife's life might be in real danger. We must stop this. You *must* cancel your planned appearance at Piccadilly.'

To her surprise Valentino just laughed.

Posie was shocked.

'You seem remarkably unconcerned, Mr Valentino,' she said coolly. 'You seem to have wanted my opinion and I will therefore give it to you: these threats look dangerous to me.'

Posie was remembering back to a time, two-and-a-half years ago, when, by chance, she had been involved in a case involving another movie star, a woman. Small-fry of course, compared to someone of Mr Valentino's world-wide standing, but a case which had been complex and dangerous nonetheless, involving infatuated stalkers. All of it had been a heady mix, with danger present at every twist and turn.

Posie shivered now, as if some old ghost had walked over her grave unhurriedly.

She adopted her best bossiest-girl-in-the-class voice, prim and knowing: 'I've dealt with stalkers before, you know. And you shouldn't be cavalier about their intentions, Mr Valentino. Although I suppose you are used to thousands of adoring women writing to you and suggesting crazy things. But this…well. I don't like it, sir. Not one little bit.'

From beneath his homburg hat, Rudolph Valentino's nearly-black eyes sparkled. He came even closer to Posie now and she inhaled that cigar smell, the minty-freshness of the man himself. The scent of powder, too; the slightly sweet stench of pan-stick.

He whispered in her ear while gesticulating at the group behind him: 'Say, Miss Parker. I think this is an inside job.'

'Oh?'

Posie frowned.

She re-read the notes, then looked up at Valentino again. Raised an eyebrow. 'I see.'

She immediately understood Poulson's summing-up of this situation as requiring a 'woman's touch'. At least, she hoped against hope that this was all that was required.

She nodded. 'Because of the reference to the Christmas lights, you mean? And also to the extreme spending on your new film? You said that both of those things were top-secret, sir?'

'Yes.'

The film star took a long drag on his cigar. 'Exactly. There must only be about two or three men in England who know about my switching on of these lights! And also, the note's got a certain amount of hostility to it, ah? Don't you think? Saying Natacha's film will be a "future pile of trash". Not many outside my current film company, Ariad, even *know* about *The Hooded Falcon*, let alone think it will be trash. These notes are obviously written by someone who is inside all of this; knows my present situation well.'

'You said this film, *The Hooded Falcon*, has been written by your wife?'

'Oh yes. *Mamma Mia!* It's her life, just now. A pet project. All she talks about.'

So the note hadn't been created as a sort of weird, wretched cry for attention by Valentino's wife herself, then.

If Natacha Rambova was proud of her as-yet-unmade film, as was being hinted at by her husband, she wouldn't be referring to it like that in a note, Posie felt sure of it.

'And Miss Naldi and yourself are due to star in this film?'

'That's right.'

So it couldn't be Miss Naldi, either, could it? An actress whose future and income might be depending on a part in *The Hooded Falcon*, and whose time was already being invested over here in Europe helping to buy the movie's props and costumes. These three people were all involved in the accusation of 'frittering money away'.

She was burning to ask the obvious question – *is the film*

going to be bad? – but it seemed more than rude, bearing in mind the personalities and sensibilities involved.

Posie looked across at the group again, who were starting to come towards the table, like moths to a flame.

Posie focused on the two men in the group. Reed Amory, Valentino's Personal Secretary, and Donald Derekson, the Manager. If this *was* an inside job, being generated to scare Valentino in some way, didn't it make sense that one of these two men might be behind it? Both might have active reasons to want to slow down or stop the spending on the film.

'What do you want me to *do*, Mr Valentino?'

'I trust you, Miss Parker. Observe this little group, ah? It *must* be one of them. Tell me what you think. Stay awhile. Chat if you can.'

He came even closer to Posie's ear and she felt the hairs on the back of her neck stand up. 'I had it in mind it was my wife, Miss Parker, when I first saw this, early this morning. Natacha is more dramatic than most actresses I know, and we're not exactly getting along all that well just now…'

'But *why* would she write such things? Horrible things?'

'Wanted me to make a fuss of her more, maybe? Wants a big police escort? When we were in Italy last year to meet my family, she was distraught that we weren't getting enough attention; no-one had heard of her, and not many had seen my films. Personally, I enjoyed the freedom, but she hated it. Maybe the way we are conducting ourselves here – undercover – has finally got too much and she wants some serious attention? It would be very like her…'

Valentino smiled. 'But she'll be disappointed with my response, if that's what she wanted. Apart from the one police contact to help with my appearance at Piccadilly tonight, which was already organised, and speaking to you, I haven't shown these notes around at all. Not even among this little group here. Now, here they all are. Let me make up a cover-story for you, Miss Parker. I don't want them to know I've gone and spoken to a private eye. It's gonna add to the tensions brewing up already. It would be a little awkward.'

Awkward!

Posie felt like laughing.

They'd better hope the notes were nothing more than awkward, too, otherwise they'd be in serious trouble, and someone would most likely end up dead.

****

Three

Time was of the essence, and Posie knew it. She let Valentino introduce her to his wife Natacha and then to Nita Naldi. Both wore very similar dropped-waisted satin evening-dresses in bright white, and were obviously already ready for the ceremony.

'Meet Miss Parker, ladies. She's gonna be taking us over to Piccadilly later, for the Lights Ceremony. She's from the London Lord Mayor's office, ah!'

Posie tried not to be star-struck, but it was hard. These two women, for they came as a pair, were young but forceful, with Natacha staring down at her in something like confusion and irritation. But she was the sour to Nita Naldi's pure sweetness, because the film star was immediately putting Posie at ease, laughing, joking, shaking hands, offering cigarettes. Her plain biscuit-coloured face was made-up as if for shooting a movie: heavy black kohl around her twinkling eyes; masses of red lipstick on a mouth which was a smidgen too big; a grosgrain hairband holding back her black, bobbed hair with its curling Marcel wave.

Natacha sat next to Valentino, proprietorially close, with Nita throwing herself down in Dolly's chair, beside Posie, ignoring the white fur coat thrown down so carelessly there.

Both of Valentino's women began to drink the champagne which Mr Poulson was flitting about the table with. The pianist on stage was playing a tinkling, easy, gorgeous number, and his partner, a dapper jazz singer, began to sing in a velvety-rich voice. The music was sonorous, perfect without being overbearing. Not too loud for conversation. In other company, Posie would have given herself up to the music.

But she was frantically studying the two other men of the company: the Personal Secretary, Reed Amory, a suntanned, extremely good-looking blonde man in his early twenties who looked like he should have been off somewhere playing tennis, and the Manager, Donald Derekson, a big, portly, sweaty, florid-faced businessman in his late forties, who looked like he'd rather be away in the sunshine or out playing golf. The men made a show of watching the stage, not drinking champagne, but smoking intently.

'You ever heard Layton & Johnstone play before, Miss Parker?' said Valentino smoothly. 'If not, you're in for a real treat.'

'Of course she ain't heard them before!' exclaimed Natacha angrily. 'A woman from an office? What's *she* gonna be doin' in here in normal circumstances?'

'Natacha!' said Valentino calmly, staring at the stage. 'Treat our guest with respect please. It costs nothing to show good manners, ah!'

Posie felt a touch of an arm. 'I'm so truly sorry,' purred Nita Naldi in her lovely American voice, but surprisingly Irish in its intonation. 'Natacha there is probably just downright jealous of you, Miss Parker.'

'*Me?*' Posie really did laugh now.

'Uh-huh. Look at you! All gorgeous, without even trying. You're the spit of Natacha, really, ain't you? Blue eyes, porcelain doll skin. And Rudy loves that look. She's jealous of the way he's sitting here with you, chatting easily, giving you his undivided attention. Probably jealous too of the baby you're having!'

Nita Naldi cast a meaningful look at Posie's belly, and sighed. 'That's all Rudy wants, you know: a family. They argue about it constantly, its tearing them apart. Natacha doesn't want a child. Not at all. Says it will get in the way of her career: the costumes, the scripts, the big new film…'

'*The Hooded Falcon*?'

'My gosh! Rudy *has* taken you into his confidence.' The actress lit a cigarette now, but smoked it without making a fuss, not using a holder at all. 'That's right. The big film.'

Posie carried on. *In for a penny, in for a pound.* 'And do you think it will be any good, this film? Are you excited about it?'

There was a slightly telling pause. Posie let the beat of the silence go on. She was good at getting information from people, people who often didn't think they would speak up.

'We-ell.' A quick flash of dark-kohled eyes rolled in the direction of Natacha, who was sitting cross-armed and surly-mouthed, muttering asides to her husband.

'Me and Natacha, we're friends, ya know? So, I can't say too much. I owe her a sort-of loyalty, although it's not watertight. And really, I'm more friendly with Rudy here himself: we've filmed a lot together. But *The Hooded Falcon* feels a bit flimsy, somehow. Tenuous, you know? And I don't think Rudy's heart is really in it. And I know Mr Derekson is getting the heebie-jeebies. He's the big blank chequebook and he was just giving Natacha there a good old warning: sayin' we'd be on our way outta here this comin' Saturday – right back to New York City on a steamboat – rather than returning to Paris tomorrow night, like we're supposed to, if she didn't quit the spending.'

'I see. And Mr Amory there, is he employed by Mr Valentino or by Ariad themselves?'

'Oh, Reed? He's Rudy's pet, and ain't he a doll? Rudy

pays him personally. I reckon Reed Amory should be in the movies himself, don't you? Yummy boy. But he's strictly hands-off! Got himself some babe called Henrietta back home in The Hamptons, and doin' very nicely for himself, thank you! He's fairly new; Rudy only hired him a week or so before we came over here to Europe, but he organises us all very nicely. He's proved very efficient.'

'How convenient.'

Posie looked at her watch. It was past four-thirty. She needed to crack on.

She smiled in a bland, jolly sort of way. 'The lights will be a big surprise, won't they? How kind of Mr Valentino to agree to it, and with such secrecy, too!'

Nita Naldi stubbed out her cigarette. 'Oh, I dunno about *secrecy*! That's Rudy's little conceit. They let him think that; Donald and all! Rudy's kinda trusting, ya know? Such a sweet fella. I reckon a fair few people know all about this lights fandango. I was left behind at The Ritz today when the Valentinos came here for lunch, then went gadding about shopping, and I heard both Don and Reed on the telephone in the lobby at various points discussin' it all! Don seemed to be inviting newspapers to come, as many as he could – good for publicity I suppose, although he never mentioned Rudy's name specifically – and Reed was on the phone to the Lord Mayor's office, discussin' boring technicalities with a boring office-type person.'

Nita Naldi simulated a mock-yawn. 'He was re-checking the exact times for the ceremony at Piccadilly, and exact locations of things, and the place for the car to wait, too. *Very* boring. Poor Reed! Can you *imagine* how boring a lot of his job must actually be? And that was all before he called the Aerodrome with some rearrangement of our tickets to be couriered over to The Ritz or some such dull business. Oh! Dull, dull, dull. How can he bear it?'

Nita Naldi suddenly looked horrified. 'Oh! But what am I saying? Maybe that was *you* on the telephone to him, at your office, all about those car technicalities and such like?'

The film star flushed a deep dark red. '*You* work for the Mayor, don't you, Miss? I sure am sorry. No disrespect intended, Ma'am. I didn't mean you or your job was boring!'

Posie laughed. 'No offence taken. It's fine.'

Nothing much was making sense here.

Friends who weren't friends. Loyalties which weren't watertight. Secrets which weren't secrets. Threats which weren't threats.

Or were they?

She wanted to speak to Natacha Valentino urgently.

But how? The girl seemed hostile. And then, as if in perfect understanding, Valentino stood up. 'I just seen someone I gotta speak to!'

And he was extricating himself from the table, disappearing off somewhere in the darkness. Posie moved into his seat seamlessly.

But before she could strike up any sort of conversation with Valentino's wife, she felt a sharp tap on her right shoulder, and a small basket was being thrust into her line of view.

Inside, on a bed of shredded sugar-paper, were all manner of utterly beautiful decorations: Christmas trees and tiny painted presents; small halo-ed angels and a golden Christmas cracker. They were palm-sized, and all of them were twinkling away merrily, blues and whites, reds, greens, silvers, pinks. Tiny, tiny electric bulbs were inside them, keeping the things flashing.

'Take one, lovey,' came a familiar cockney voice in her ear. 'All of you, take one. Pass the basket on, eh? Compliments of the house! The Café de Paris always hands out electric favours: it's normally little cats and dancin' girls, but of course, it's nearly Christmas, innit?'

It was Dolly, who now appeared completely sober and pulled-together, eyes large but focused, smiling knowingly at Posie, one eyebrow raised. Playing along. Not letting the side down.

Posie pulled out a Christmas tree. It was perfect for showing to Phyllis later. The little girl would be utterly transfixed.

Natacha Valentino picked up a favour without looking at it, frowning in Dolly's direction, as Dolly went gamely on around the table to the two men, who were drinking coffees which had just arrived.

'Who's *that*?' said Natacha sourly. 'The little London match-girl?'

She just happens to be a Countess, and worth a thousand of you, thought Posie to herself angrily, but she said nothing, merely flicking the small tree favour's lights on and off in an excitable manner.

'It's all about electric light today, isn't it?' she said breezily. Natacha Valentino looked at Posie as if she were a dimwit, then shrugged.

'I suppose so.'

'Are you excited about your husband's surprise appearance to turn on the London Christmas lights?'

Another shrug, non-committal. 'Should I be?'

'It will be unforgettable, surely. Some might find it frightening! New technology…' Posie pushed on regardless, trying hard to remember the exact details of the first note, the right order of the words.

'Some might think it was dangerous. Those Christmas angels in a blaze of electric glory.'

She studied the girl's blank face; the confused blue eyes. The complete lack of understanding there. She knew Natacha had been an actress upon occasion, but if she knew something about that note, the wording, then this was acting on another level, for she looked completely baffled.

'I'm sorry? What's gonna be dangerous? You tellin' me something I don't know, lady?'

'Golly, no. Just general observations. I'm just excited, you can tell!'

'Mnnn. I'll be excited when it's over and done with, that's all.'

'I understand you have important business here in London, Mrs Valentino. Buying items for your exciting new film. You've written it and you're going to produce it, too, aren't you? That's fabulous! A breakthrough, surely? So exciting that a woman will be taking charge of a Hollywood movie, controlling nearly all aspects of the production…'

The girl looked momentarily at ease, happy. Pleased at Posie's assessment of things.

'That's right. Yes, it is a breakthrough, and kind of you to say so. It will start being filmed in about one month's time.'

Here was the ice breaking, the thaw coming. Natacha Valentino was obviously genuinely proud of her planned project. Too proud to ever call it 'trash'.

No, the wife was a non-starter here as far as those notes were concerned, Posie concluded. *Nothing doing.*

Tinkly silver laughter floated over, and Dolly, on the arm of a much taller, black-haired young woman sporting a very short blunt bob, strolled past. Dolly tapped Posie smartly on the back.

'Message from a London match-girl, Miss. Telephone. You're wanted. Over on that wall, in the booth in the recess. See?'

'Oh, thank you! It might be the Mayor. Please excuse me…'

It had been a ruse of Valentino's, Posie knew that, and stumbling in the shady dark of the space near the curving wall, Posie almost felt her way by touch towards the booth. Next to it was Valentino, smoking, hat well down.

'Say, what you got for me, Miss Parker?'

She blew out her breath, exhaled heavily. Stood against the wall. It was cosy there actually, looking out at the whole club while they couldn't see you. Like a voyeur.

'I don't think it's your wife, sir, and not Miss Naldi. I haven't spoken to your Personal Secretary or your Manager, but it actually seems ludicrous that they would send notes like that. It's in their interests, especially Mr Derekson's, that you attend the lights ceremony today, for both the money and publicity. He seems to want the press there; he might secure payments for exclusive pictures or stories, mightn't he? Try and recoup what you've been spending in Europe. And Mr Amory has apparently been carefully organising this all. He seems very efficient, with not a detail left to chance. Surely it would be counterproductive for either man to try and scare you off, after all the work they've so obviously put in?'

'Besides,' Valentino nodded, 'I trust the fellas. So where does that lead us? Precisely nowhere, I think, ah!'

With me ringing my husband and getting him to come here, pretty quickly, Posie was about to say.

But then, as if things couldn't get any odder, she caught sight of her old foe, Chief Inspector Oats.

He was making his way, completely incongruously, across the crowded dance floor, a scrubby flash of dirty beige trench-coat moving in among all the silks and satins like an ostrich in among a flock of swans.

He was looking about from side to side, pulling at his ratty moustache as he went, his blue cod-like eyes almost rolling in disbelief. Oats would hate this set-up, thought Posie firmly to herself.

Toffs! Rich people enjoying themselves when they could be out earning an honest wage!

But he would probably be happy to recount the details of the movie star and Valentino's group later – in disparaging tones – to anyone who would listen back at the Yard. And his wife, the dreadful Mrs Matilda Oats, a movie fan through and through, would dine out on this story and its reflected glory for years to come.

Posie sighed. 'I think this may be your police top-dog

on his way to meet you, Mr Valentino. His name is Chief Inspector Oats.'

'Perfect.' Valentino smiled. 'Say, I'm sure we won't need him anyhow, but nice all the same, ah!'

'Mnnn,' muttered Posie, entering the telephone booth quickly and dialling the number for New Scotland Yard, asking for her husband.

This was all turning into – as Inspector Oats would no doubt say himself in only a couple of minutes – *a mare's nest*.

Sure as bread was bread.

****

Four

'Sorry? *Who*, darling?'

'You heard me, Richard. I'm not repeating myself. As it is, I'm talking quite loudly over the sound of this music, and I'm scared I'm going to be overheard.'

She'd explained it all in a nutshell to Richard, who, as Chief Commissioner of New Scotland Yard, was probably the one man in London who would have the necessary manpower and contacts behind him to ensure that tonight's ceremony didn't turn into a full-scale disaster.

A murder in the London lights.

'What the *deuce*?'

She heard her husband groan, and imagined him standing at his desk, telephone receiver clamped to one ear, raking through his thick red hair with his other hand, in his turret of a room at New Scotland Yard, looking out the window with its view of the darkening, snow-filled evening; the twinkling lights of the Embankment and the dark, endless snake of the River Thames flowing far below.

'It's about the worst possible timing, darling. I've been in this Yearly Review all week long, and it's winding up today. That's why I took so long to answer the bally telephone: I was chairing the meeting. It must also be why Oats has got himself involved. You said this all came about on Monday?

This invitation for Valentino to turn on the lights? And the Mayor of London, eh? That's Sir Alfred Bower. Nice fella. Hmnn. I'd better speak with him directly, eh?'

Posie could picture Richard nodding, his green eyes troubled. 'Yes, I told all the Chief Inspectors beneath me to deal with problems as they arose; not to trouble me. And it seems Oats got handed this hot potato.'

Another groan came down the line. 'He's the *last* man I'd want dealing with it really. If this goes wrong this will ruin me. It will be sensational. My career will be over.'

'It's just possible a woman's life may be over, darling.'

'Of course. Yes, of course.' She sensed her husband snapping into action, now back in control.

Posie heard him giving quick, sharp orders to someone in his office, covering the receiver with his hand, muffling the exact words. Then he was back with her, clear, snappy.

'I'm going to telephone the Lord Mayor now, and speak to Sir Alfred about the details; how it's going to be organised at Piccadilly tonight. I won't give any sort of indication that I'm worried about anything other than logistics. Won't mention these odd notes. But we need to make bally certain that if this thing goes ahead, we're covering Valentino and his wife properly. You say she's got no idea?'

'That's right. She seems innocent of the thing. He hasn't told anyone in his immediate group.'

'Foolish of the fella to disregard this, eh?'

'I think he's quite trusting, Richard. Thinks it's a bit of a joke. Explained it to me as probably being a cry wolf on behalf of his own wife, who seems needy and perhaps insecure. He's pretty sure it's an inside job.'

She sighed. 'Can you get here?'

'That's what I'm going to do as soon as I've spoken to Sir Alfred. I need to ascertain how many people they imagine will be at Piccadilly Circus for this switching on the lights malarkey, and maybe revise how many police we need there to cover it; maybe even get the mounted police in. I'll speed over to you in a motor in a few minutes, and I'll have Fox and Smallbone with me. Good grief! Eros at Piccadilly, you say? You couldn't choose a busier spot, could you? Talk about needle in a haystack territory.'

'Indeed.'

'And for goodness' sake, darling, if you *do* happen to get caught up in it all and I'm not there, make sure you stand well away from Valentino, and his wife. Please take care.'

'Mnnn.'

Coming out of the booth, Posie almost bumped into the sizeable person of Donald Derekson in the dim light. He was busy shaking out a match, inhaling on a fat cigar.

'Oh! Dear me! I'm so sorry.'

'Don't be, Miss. You're a movie fan yourself?' He blew out a lot of smoke. 'Only I saw you talking to Miss Naldi back there; looked like you were enjoying yourself?'

Posie smiled tightly. In truth she hadn't yet seen one of Nita Naldi's films, and she decided honesty was the best course of action. 'Well, actually I am a fan of Mr Valentino, sir, and Miss Naldi was able to throw some interesting light on their work together.'

The man leered unpleasantly. Donald Derekson was sweating heavily, mopping at his brow with a red and white spotted handkerchief, his small brown eyes dancing backwards and forwards across the club floor, on beyond Posie.

'Ah, yes. Their work *together*. Some of us find it hard to believe the lovely Miss Naldi is happy that their romance exists only on-screen.'

Posie stiffened. She cast a glance over at the table she had been sitting at, at Nita Naldi, who had shimmied up into Posie's own spot and was touching Valentino on the arm easily, laughing uproariously at something he'd just said. Natacha Valentino was stiff, sullen; her back ramrod-straight on his other side.

'I was given to understand that Miss Naldi is a great pal of Mrs Valentino,' Posie said smoothly. 'And she was here on this buying tour for moral support as much as for anything?'

'Say what? No. Don't you believe it!'

Derekson took another big lungful of smoke. 'Mark my words, Nita Naldi has come on this wretchedly awful spending-spree for one reason only: to be with Rudy. *Rudy, Rudy, Rudy*. She wants what she can't have. She don't work for my film company, Ariad, but even so, those two are box-office dynamite. Anyone can see it! They look so good together. Off-screen too. I wish they'd get together for real. I'd sign her up right away if that happened. It would be a lovely story, a real-life romance. Financially lucrative, too. A Manager's dream! Rudy's easy, free, happy with Nita. Look at the guy! When he's with Natacha he's scared stiff: scared of her silences and her cross-patch face; scared of doing the wrong thing.'

The man sighed. 'It's a crying shame, but what can we do? We have to pander to Natacha's every whim, like this new film, just to keep Rudy on side. We can't just magic Natacha Valentino away, can we? Much as some of us would like to!'

No, but she could be 'got rid of', Posie thought to herself quickly, nervously.

'I'll be seeing you then, Miss.'

She watched the Manager amble back to the table.

Posie found she was twisting the small Christmas tree favour in her hands, snapping the lights on and off, almost without realising it, thinking hard.

NOW NATACHA VALENTINO WILL BE CAUGHT IN A BLAZE.

Hadn't the Manager, Derekson, basically just admitted the tour they were on was 'frittering money away', and he'd given a reason – a good commercial one – for wanting Natacha out of the way.

So those notes *could* have come from him, surely?

But he'd also thrown in as an aside a strong reason – if it were true – as to why Nita Naldi might want her so-called friend out of the way, too. A romantic aspect to things, a complicated twist.

She leant back against the cool wall again. Posie watched Chief Inspector Oats at the table. He was like a fish out of water, but was holding his own, sitting with Reed Amory, going step-by-step through a plan which he had brought along.

The Personal Secretary certainly seemed to know his stuff, and Oats appeared calm and organised, although he, of course, was completely unaware of the existence of the threat letters, as was, apparently, Reed Amory himself. Maybe both she and Richard were being overtly critical of Oats? Maybe he was the best man for the job, after all?

Suddenly Posie caught sight of Dolly, and she grinned to herself.

From where she was standing, Posie could see right into the wings off the stage. In the wings Dolly, bright in her white clothes, was laughing hysterically with the very young girl with the black bob. Both were dancing now – of sorts. Dolly was copying the young woman who was swinging her long arms and legs in a very strange way, arms outstretched, palms flat, in a series of jerky, but very fast movements.

'What on *earth*…' muttered Posie, astounded.

A familiar, courteous, polite voice spoke in her ear. 'It's a revolutionary dance, Miss. The Charleston. All the rage in America, you know.'

Mr Poulson was smiling slightly indulgently at the pair dancing in the wings. 'And that there is the seventeen-year-old Miss Louise Brooks, fresh off the boat from New York to show London how it's done. I can't say it's exactly my cup of tea, but by tomorrow, the Café de Paris will be a talking-point because of it. The first place in London where it was danced. The dance craze will be all over the country within days. We've booked her here until past Christmas.'

'I say! How thrilling for you!'

'It is, Miss Parker.'

And he was off again; carrying mounds of white furs and crushed white velvet scarves in his arms.

As she watched, Posie saw Poulson approach Valentino's table, handing the huge, puffy clouds of white fur to each of Nita Naldi and Natacha Valentino. He seemed to bow down before them.

The women allowed him to help them on with these snow-white, impossibly fluffy coats, to wrap themselves in the luxuriant wraps, and up on the stage Layton & Johnstone started up another number, a jolly rolling tune called 'Josephine'. While Posie was watching all of this unfold, she suddenly felt a little kick inside.

'Oh!'

And then again.

A furry of tiny kicks came suddenly, stronger than before, more like a heartbeat than anything else.

How thrilling! My baby likes music, Posie thought to herself with pleasure.

Good music too.

Or maybe he or she just wants to remind me to calm down, to get through this strange situation in one piece.

A movement at her side, a scent of an expensive woody-scented cologne, and the tall, handsome Reed Amory almost barged into her.

'Say, I didn't see you in the darkness there, Ma'am! Sorry!'

Posie saw that Inspector Oats had moved around the table awkwardly to speak directly to the ever-polite Valentino, waving the plan he had brought along right in the movie star's face.

Posie smiled at Reed Amory and the Personal Secretary grinned at her. 'Don't mind me. I just need the telephone booth here for a second, Ma'am. Long-distance call, you know how it is.'

Well, not really.

He smiled again, and his brilliant white teeth flashed at her from his suntanned face. Really, the man was seriously handsome. Like Nita Naldi had said, *he* could be a movie star, no doubt about it.

How could she gain this man's confidence?

She found herself suddenly simpering, ridiculously:

'It must be wonderful working for Mr Valentino. Is it?'

'It's not all bad, Ma'am! In fact, it's pretty good.'

Posie ploughed on. 'But I suppose you must get some odd people hanging about sometimes?' Posie shivered dramatically. 'You hear about stalkers, don't you? Mad fans?'

Reed Amory looked slightly suspicious for a moment, then laughed good-naturedly: 'We do sometimes get odd folk, yeah. But most times it's all pretty good. The thing is, you have to make sure you don't get paranoid in this job. Like this morning, at The Ritz, I saw this huge fat guy in a loud pin-striped suit at the Reception, just before Mr Valentino was due to leave the building. The guy was hanging about and I convinced myself he was there to make a nuisance for Mr Valentino, a journalist or a crazy fella, maybe. But the guy actually seemed very respectable and so I did nothing. Just watched. After a bit he disappeared. So, I'm wrong sometimes, I guess. That's what I mean about paranoia. Now, if you'll excuse me…'

Posie frowned. Something the Personal Secretary had just said made her feel uncomfortable; had sent alarm bells ringing somehow, but just at this moment she couldn't for the life of her think why.

And then he'd pulled the cubicle door shut, pulled the baize curtain over.

Posie lingered on, tried her best to listen, but only heard a muttered request for a connection, and the name 'Henrietta' mentioned. Wasn't that the girlfriend Nita

Naldi had mentioned? Based somewhere on the East Coast of America? Posie checked her watch. It must be nearly lunchtime there now.

She was about to move away and give the man some real privacy when she heard another voice in her ear, but a beloved one this time.

'Posie?'

She turned quickly, grinning. 'Darling! I didn't see you come in!'

Richard Lovelace, dark battered homburg hat still on, smiled briefly. Posie could tell he was in too much of a fluster for a kiss, for the news about the kick, for any niceties.

'We were allowed down that handy Rupert Street entrance, the one they save for pretty much Royalty alone, it seems. Poulson is a good man.'

Posie looked at her watch. It was twenty-past five, and she saw how Inspector Oats was scouring the place for the Secretary, Reed Amory, who darted out of the telephone cubicle as if on cue and joined Oats, tapping at his own watch, indicating the door. Valentino was shrugging on his own huge, expensive coat, nodding at both the white-clad women with him.

We should be leaving now.

Posie caught sight of Sergeant Fox, tall and blonde and angular-looking, leaning against the darkness of the wall, flicking urgently through a pile of newspapers, and then Smallbone, shorter, darker, with his fashionable moustache, sidling along to get a good view of the party at the table. He disappeared quickly, however, into the vacant telephone booth.

'What did you find out, darling?' Posie whispered to her husband, as they watched the women at the table drinking up, clapping the musicians, painfully slow to hurry.

'I just caught Sir Alfred at his offices. We'll see him again in a bit, all undercover of course. He gives rather a different story to your pal Rudolph over there.'

'Oh?'

'Sir Alfred explained that a good deal of freebies were asked for. And then the Manager himself – Derekson, is it? –suggested Valentino as a surprise guest for this event. Derekson said he'd read about how the new Christmas lights would be switched on this week, and that surely having a famous American movie star to do that would take it up another level? All for a nicely-negotiated fat fee, of course.'

Posie rolled her eyes. 'I see. That makes sense.'

She looked at Derekson's ham-like florid neck, at his ungainly tilting moves as he wrapped a bright red scarf about himself. 'So the Manager kept that fact from Valentino. Clever. Got Valentino to believe his appearance would be for free, as a favour. Valentino also believed it was his Personal Secretary who had organised the whole thing.'

Lovelace shrugged. 'Does it matter? The Personal Secretary and the Manager are both responsible for keeping the show on the road, aren't they? So to speak. Perhaps they work together on some things. Who is who, anyhow?'

Posie pointed the men out, and Lovelace nodded, looking suddenly slightly confused, as if someone in Valentino's crowd had at one stage been familiar to him.

Then he seemed to convince himself he was mistaken, shrugged slightly and carried on: 'Whatever the case, Sir Alfred agreed to the suggestion, and has paid up. He consulted his own office and they all thought it was a brilliant idea.'

'So, a good many people know about Valentino's appearance, then? If there was an office discussion about it?'

'I imagine so. Although this was all agreed on Monday and it's remained a tightly-kept secret until now. That's what Sir Alfred wanted; to create maximum impact on the night itself. A big surprise for Londoners. It was an agreement between him and the Manager.'

Fox was quickly beside them both, and in his hands he was holding a small stack of newspapers. He waved an evening edition of *The Times* at them both. 'Well, I'd say this was a secret which has been carefully leaked, sir. For maximum excitement value. These are the evening papers.'

He shook out the front page. It read:

MYSTERY GUEST TO SWITCH LONDON'S FIRST CHRISTMAS LIGHTS ON! ALL IS REVEALED INSIDE!

Posie grabbed at the newspaper, flicked to the second page. '*They* think here it will be the Prince of Wales turning on the lights! Now he's back from gallivanting around America. Pah! But it's interesting that they've got wind of the fact *someone* famous might be involved, isn't it?'

She remembered Nita Naldi telling her Mr Derekson had been calling newspapers from the lobby of The Ritz. 'This could be part of Valentino's Manager's scheme of whipping up interest in the event? I think he was trying to get press coverage, but I was told he gave no names away. He must have been honouring the agreement. Maybe the press have just reached their own conclusions?'

Fox raised an eyebrow and, like some magician pulling out rabbits from a hat, pulled out yet another newspaper. This was *The Post*.

Their headline was nearer the mark by far.

GLAMOROUS CHRISTMAS LIGHTS MYSTERY GUEST IS A MOVIE STAR! RUMOURED TO BE 'THE KID' – CHARLIE CHAPLIN!

'And look at this,' Fox said softly.

He pulled out the *Associated Press*. 'They think it's an American star, too. There's a tentative suggestion it could be Douglas Fairbanks. But they're not certain enough to say for sure.'

Fox shook out his last newspaper.

It was *The City News*. 'And look here, these fella's have hit the nail on the head!'

Posie read the headline.

OUTSIDE CHANCE THAT LIGHTS WILL BE SWITCHED ON TONIGHT BY 'THE SHEIK'! IS RUDY VALENTINO IN TOWN?

'Golly!' Posie frowned, her heart beating faster. 'They've got it in one! Someone has told them for sure. But it's as if someone has been serving all the newspapers up with tit-bits of information, isn't it? Dropping names? *Different* names. But why? Whipping up a frenzy? I'm not sure that's quite Mr Derekson's style, somehow…'

Fox, looking perplexed, nodded. 'Well, all I know is that right now all of London is talking about it. There are crowds forming at Piccadilly Circus, and, under revised emergency instructions, banks of bobbies are lining the streets, both along Regent Street itself and lining Piccadilly right up to Green Park. We don't dare bring out the mounted police, as we've been told the sudden electric lights might cause the horses to bolt and run.'

Fox looked exasperated. 'We've tried ringing the lads at *The City News* but they won't speak about their source as to the Valentino story. I've told Smallbone to investigate a bit and telephone your friendly newspaper contact, Miss Parker.'

'Sam Stubbs, at the *Associated Press*?'

'That's right. He's Editor there now, Miss. Quite the man. Helpful, too. If all the newspapers have been drip-fed news, he's likely to know *who* did it, and *what* was said, exactly. He'll know how he came by his front page story, surely?'

Lovelace was pleased. 'Good work, Sergeant. I must speak briefly to Mr Valentino, see these threatening notes. I need to explain to him that his cover may well be blown too, and that we've upped his protection levels because of it. Give me that copy of *The City News*, won't you, Fox? Can you get him over here, Posie? The last thing I want to do is make a scene out in the open, it would embarrass Oats, for one thing. Much the best thing is if Oats gets on with it all alone, thinks he's in charge. Then I'll "blend" in, as much as I can. But I'm not letting you out of my sight, Posie love. No way.'

Posie managed to convince Valentino to come with her, which he did with an eager, easy grace, buttoning up his luxuriously huge shearling coat, which made him appear as wide as it did tall. She left him speaking to Richard near the telephone booth, pulling out those two cut-newspaper notes from his wallet in a guarded surreptitious manner, and then she went to get Dolly.

She saw how Natacha and Nita Naldi were ready: taking the opportunity to re-do their red, red lipsticked mouths. Each had jammed on a white matching turban.

Posie found Dolly easily and she persuaded her to come along.

'Cor, lovey! You got yerself some jazzy little new pals now, ain't you? I 'ad to stop my jaw from fallin' on the floor when I caught sight of *him*! But all credit to yer, lovey! He's as nice as pie, ain't he? *The Sheik*… Oh! I could eat him up, he's that lovely! Lucky, lucky wife of his. Where did you say we were goin' now, lovey? Lights, you say? Outside, is it? I need my coat then, don't I?'

And Dolly looped back to the table and picked up the priceless white fur off the back of a chair, made an elaborate show of putting it on, much to the consternation of Natacha Valentino, who looked absolutely revolted. Because now Dolly and she looked almost identical, and it obviously rankled.

Natacha was playing with one of the Christmas tree electric favours and she snapped the thing down on the table with an aggravated bang.

Nita Naldi nodded politely at Dolly, obviously realising that she was a person of quite some standing, after all. 'You sure look very nice, Miss. I like the necklace, too.'

'Not bad for a match-girl, eh?' said Dolly, cheerily, also putting on some scarlet lipstick. 'Sold a lot of matches for this little outfit, I'm tellin' yer!'

Posie could never compete with this level of fashion, even under normal circumstances.

She was wearing Richard's second-best tweed coat again, Poulson having appeared with it as if by magic.

'The Rupert Street exit, I think,' Mr Poulson said discreetly to Reed Amory, who simply nodded and turned tail, indicating everyone in the group should follow him.

Posie was aware of Valentino up ahead, joining his Personal Secretary again, linking arms with the man, having finished talking to Richard. Valentino was grinning that melting-heart smile, pulling his hat further down.

She saw Richard and Fox in the shadow of the wall, observing everything.

Posie moved to join them, but just at that moment a very small Christmas tree favour in Natacha Valentino's hands popped loudly and caught ablaze.

Natacha dropped the thing in a flurry of rising flames right by the staircase they were about to ascend, and she screamed aloud in pure terror.

****

Five

It had taken a few minutes for the hysterical girl to calm down, with Mr Poulson offering soothing platitudes, and Inspector Oats actually seeming sympathetic for once.

When it was established that Natacha Valentino was unhurt, and that the tiny Christmas tree favour had probably just malfunctioned, the group started to move down Rupert Street, moving on to Coventry Street, with Inspector Oats leading the brigade.

He was followed by Valentino, who was surrounded on either side by his Manager and Personal Secretary, with the two American women in white behind, and Posie and Dolly at the back, flanked by Richard Lovelace and Sergeant Fox.

Posie's thoughts were scrambling.

NOW NATACHA VALENTINO WILL BE CAUGHT IN A BLAZE.

Well: she nearly had been caught in a horrible blaze just now, hadn't she? Or had that been the most awful coincidence?

Whatever the explanation, there was no way Posie would be handing her own small favour over to Richard's beloved daughter Phyllis to play with.

As she walked Posie was going over in her mind

those newspaper headlines from this evening's editions which Fox had brought to her attention, with their varied suggestions as to who might be switching on the lights: the Prince of Wales; Charlie Chaplin; Douglas Fairbanks. A small, outside chance it was Valentino…

He'd been so careful about keeping out of the limelight, and he wasn't here filming, or on a big, well-advertised publicity trip. Nor on a holiday either. Most of the time Valentino was in New York, or Hollywood, where he lived, or, more recently, in Paris.

So, unless prompted, most newspaper editors and the general public would have assumed that Valentino was in one of those places.

Someone, somewhere had definitely let on.

But why? And was it connected to the notes?

Posie tripped along the salted-snowy-slushy streets in her not-very-practical Mary-Janes, wishing longingly for her sturdy black snow-boots which she kept in her office at Grape Street, for weather exactly like this.

She barely noticed the crowds massing on the street's pavements like one black heaving monster, people clad in dingy raincoats and wet-weather gear, desperate for a glimpse of light and glamour; of anything more hopeful than their own lives.

She took in a blurry line of injured and maimed men – Great War veterans – begging on mats of damp cardboard outside the cafés and restaurants which famously lined this street. Dirty slush edged the pavements and snowflakes were still falling heavily.

Posie noticed that the normal street-lamps were not on, and all the light in the dark of the evening was coming out of the huge arched windows set in the grey-stone buildings which lined the road: cinemas, theatres, shops, the Trocadero Restaurant.

One cinema was advertising a film called *Blood and Sand* with the title picked out in dazzling white bulbs, and with double life-sized posters stuck up one after the other for an entire run of windows. To Posie's shock, she saw the dark eyes of Valentino staring out at her from these windows, again and again as she walked by, dressed gaudily as a bull-fighter, clasping a red cloak, holding onto a woman with a dark chignon and polka-dot, Spanish clothes. *Nita Naldi*.

Posie looked ahead to the backs of these two real-life movie stars walking with the snow falling upon them, seemingly unconcerned and unruffled at the prospect of walking past giant versions of themselves.

It must be a daily occurrence, she thought to herself, with not one little smidgen of envy.

What an odd life.

Lovelace had been busy talking in undertones to Sergeant Fox, and now he was joined by an excitable Constable Smallbone, who bounded up behind them all, squeezing through the crowds. 'Guv'nor! Sir!'

'Pipe down, lad.' Lovelace looked cross, chanced a glance at Inspector Oats up way ahead, but he was reassured he still hadn't been seen.

'What is it, Constable?'

Smallbone was like a terrier on the scent. 'I spoke to Sam Stubbs,' he said, in a growl, under his breath. 'And he said he'd received a telephone call today, before the evening edition was due to go to press, about three-thirty. A woman told him that a surprise guest – one of the world's most famous men – would be turning on the London lights tonight! She hinted it was Douglas Fairbanks.'

'A *woman*?' said Posie, startled. 'Are you sure?'

'Yes, Miss. Stubbs was certain of it: took the call himself. Insisted on it as it involved changing the front page. She sounded local apparently, London accent, but *cheap*. East End.'

''Ere! You callin' me "cheap" 'cos I'm from the East End, an' all?' rasped Dolly, who was walking along smoking one of her usual Sobranies, laughing uproariously.

'Sorry, Lady Cardigeon. No offence meant.'

'Oh, none taken, laddie.'

Smallbone rushed on. 'Stubbs was obviously wanting to corroborate the story, and Lord Alfred, the Mayor, wasn't giving anything away. But when he rang around the other editors on all the other major papers, he found they'd all been fed similar stories by a similar-sounding woman, but some had other names – the Prince of Wales, and Chaplin, and our Valentino here – given out specifically. Those papers had all decided to go to print, and Stubbs felt he'd be on the back foot if he didn't, so he thought he'd better join them with his take on things.'

'Publish or be damned, eh?' muttered Lovelace. Ahead of them, all of the circular ring road around the statue of Eros had been closed to traffic, and heavy, swollen crowds were being held back by rings of policemen.

'It doesn't make sense.' Posie shook her head. 'There *is* no local East End London girl. Unless this was Natacha – she's certainly worked as an actress in the past. But at three-thirty she was buying up half of Liberty's Cruise Collection. I saw her with my own eyes!'

'Miss Naldi, then?' queried Fox, blonde eyebrow raised. 'She *is* an actress. A fine one too.'

Posie laughed. 'But she's a silent movie actress. We have no idea if she can 'do' accents!' Posie bit at her lip. 'Although at around three-thirty she was sitting pretty in The Ritz Hotel, the lounge, I think. So, she *could* have done it. Could have placed the calls.'

But the words sounded hollow to her ears, and it didn't somehow ring true.

'But it gets more interesting, sir,' ploughed on Smallbone in an urgent whisper. 'Listen! Sam Stubbs published anyway, thinking he'd join his fellow London editors in sinking or swimming. And then he thought of other ways to try and verify the story about the mystery guest.'

'But how could he possibly do that?' Lovelace had taken

Posie firmly by the arm now, and was steering her carefully along the icy pavement, while up ahead Oats had stopped abruptly and was speaking to his charges, motioning towards the statue in the centre of the place. He was a man fighting without weapons, against an enemy he was unaware of, and Posie, probably for the first time ever, felt sorry for the man.

Smallbone grinned. 'Stubbs started telephoning around the bookies, sir. Harry Ogden were carrying the story as their main event today. They were offering odds of 10/1 for the Prince of Wales to turn on the lights, sir, and 20/1 on Charlie Chaplin.'

Lovelace whistled. 'So the bookies were believing the stories? They'd have to, eh? To offer odds like those.'

Smallbone grinned. 'Exactly, sir.'

Lovelace bit at his lip, looking momentarily confused.

Oats, ahead, had seen him at last and flashed a stoic but disappointed grimace in Lovelace's direction, gesturing that the party was stepping inside a discreet doorway, right next to the Piccadilly Underground Station, and next to the traffic lights which led across to the snow-capped Eros statue.

Posie saw the door led to a small, plain but decent little café, right under the famous billboards reading 'VIM' and 'BOVRIL' and 'SCHWEPPES GINGER ALE'. They headed there, Lovelace digging something out from his pocket as he walked.

Posie saw it was the two notes sent to Valentino. Lovelace was frantically scanning them over and over, looking for something or anything which might help. But finding nothing.

'Sir? Chief Commissioner?'

'Wait…'

'Sir, this is important.'

A sigh. 'Go on, Smallbone.'

Thumps and arms and elbows and a mad crush of people seemed to invade them.

'There was something else Stubbs found out, sir. A bookies called Raddisons in Covent Garden were quoting odds of 500/1 on Rudolph Valentino being the mystery guest who would turn on the Christmas lights tonight!'

'*What?* Odds of 500/1! That's crazy. It means if you knew it was him, and knew of this bet, you could clean up!'

'Yes, sir. I've checked and they are taking a fair few bets now, not thousands mind, but a few biggies, all based on the cover of *The City News*.'

Lovelace nodded: 'It also means Raddisons must have known Valentino was in town to offer the odds in the first place, but strongly believed he wouldn't actually end up being the mystery guest. Odd, very odd.'

'But where does this lead us?' hissed Fox as they crushed through the crowds outside the café, and moved inside.

'Precisely nowhere!' muttered Lovelace in exasperation.

A big clock on the wall inside said it was ten to six. And Posie saw now that this place had been selected on purpose. Booked out most probably by the Lord Mayor as a place to enable privacy for the film star, and to gain a few moments of calm before the crush of people tried to mob Valentino outside.

The entire group were gathered here, a tiny dainty waitress in smart black was bobbing about with trays of champagne flutes, looking like she might drop them all.

The Mayor, a small, slight, good-looking man in his early fifties with a full head of thick white hair, was wearing his big crimson velvet dress capes, with the huge gold chains of office glinting in the bright white lights of this clean, small place.

He was shaking hands and beaming at Valentino, who had taken off his hat at last, the strong harsh lights illuminating that famous face, and the orange pan-stick didn't seem that orange here at all. Just about perfect, in fact.

A middle-aged woman with thick shingled grey hair

and wearing emerald-green velvet was laughing along sweetly at the Mayor's side. His wife, Posie guessed.

Oats was introducing everyone to the Mayor: Donald Derekson and Nita Naldi and then finally Natacha Valentino, the last two women looking striking in their identical white get-up. Like two American dreams.

The Personal Secretary, Reed, was motioning out of the door, towards the waiting crowds. He was speaking to a tall woman wearing drab black with a white paper frothy cap, the Proprietress of this fortunate little café which had tonight been touched by such wonderful magic.

Posie heard Reed's lovely accent, saw a flash of the white sparkling teeth. 'Ten minutes, that's all, Miss. There'll be no hanging around.'

He took a flute of champagne and smiled across at Posie, who nodded back.

Dolly was leaning against a chrome stool, not smoking and not drinking, which was unusual. She tapped Lovelace on the shoulder. 'Let me look at those notes you was just so engrossed in, Richard.'

And he did as he was told, for once. Huffily handing them over, blocking them from view.

'What is it, Dolls?' asked Posie, scanning her friend's face.

Dolly jabbed at the first note. 'Thought so!' she trilled. 'These are from a French paper, see? See this word "VALENTINO"? Well, if you look carefully, you'll see the French accent has been cut off one of the 'E's. And again, down here. And this pink newspaper paper which is bein' used; it's not exactly English, is it?'

Posie always forgot that Dolly's mother had been French, and her friend therefore spoke the language fluently, although it was seldom mentioned and even less practised.

'*French*!' hissed Posie at Richard. 'They've just come over from France. Yesterday. Arrived at Croydon Aerodrome from Paris.'

'What are you saying, Posie?' asked Lovelace, exchanging carefully-guarded nods with the Mayor.

'I'm saying Poulson was right, and so was Mr Valentino. It's an inside job. It's French newsprint paper which was brought over here from Paris yesterday and been cut and pasted onto plain English white postcards; bought in town last night or very early this morning. So it's definitely one of this group, isn't it?'

'Hmnn.'

'Time, everyone!' exclaimed the Mayor proudly and the Proprietress opened the glass door of the café, peering out, and Posie looked at her briefly and then saw that outside there were banks and banks of photographers, and reporters, and flash-lights were now going off, the tang of the flash chalky in the frozen, snowy air.

'*Who is it? Who is it?*' screamed the crowds, and the cameras were popping and clicking regardless.

'*Who is the mystery guest?*'

The two American women in their furs stepped out first, all ready to be adored and gasped at.

A red carpet had been laid out, marking a short but fantastical walk over the road to Eros at the centre of his island in the snow.

Posie and Dolly hung back, Lovelace with his arm barring their exit.

The Mayor walked out now, beaming, wife on his arm, raising his free arm in a wave, to loud applause. And then behind him, hat off, shoulders down, relaxed, walked Valentino. Smiling, a cigar in his hand, cool as a cucumber.

There were gasps and shouts, screams.

'*It's Valentino! Rudolph Valentino! The Sheik! It's The Sheik!*'

Oats together with Fox and Smallbone were following, protecting. Posie walked behind Lovelace, barely hearing the Mayor's introduction to the assembled crowds, his proud words of welcome, his gesture to Rudolph Valentino, at his side.

They were all now on that island, next to the statue.

Posie saw a black box, set up by the Eros, a big silver lever like a gearstick at its centre. She remembered those words: *YOU THINK YOU'RE SO SMART LIGHTING UP THOSE CHRISTMAS ANGELS IN A BLAZE OF ELECTRIC GLORY, DON'T YOU?*

Rudolph Valentino *was* smart, and trusting, and kind. A lovely man with a lovely smile.

Faced with ragged chants of *'The Sheik! It's the Sheik!'* he was doing a good job of waving and grinning and turning from side to side so his adoring fans could get a good view; the women of the crowd growing increasingly hysterical, not quite believing that a movie star was in their midst, let alone *this* one.

Posie looked briefly at Lovelace, and his eyes were clouded with worry, a frown creasing his forehead. He was scanning the crowds, anxious.

Needle in a haystack territory.

Posie moved even closer, heard a sudden hush come over the place. She listened to Rudolph Valentino talk in his beautiful, usually never-heard voice, slightly muffled in the snow, heard him describe how wonderful London was, what an honour it had been to be asked here tonight for the first ever turning on of the Christmas lights.

Posie hurried to stand next to Natacha, recalling the horrible words: *NOW NATACHA VALENTINO WILL BE CAUGHT IN A BLAZE.*

'Posie! No!' Richard's voice was nervous behind her.

She was aware of Dolly at her side, like a shadow. She saw Valentino nod at the Mayor, and dark-boiler-suited men, electricians presumably, darted away expectantly to ensure all ran smoothly.

Valentino put his hand on the silver lever of the black box. Everyone was facing Regent Street, the darkness.

He pulled his hand back, and everyone cheered, roared.

* * * *

Six

Regent Street and Piccadilly Circus itself were suddenly thrown into a dazzling display of brightness.

Bells and tiny glittering chains of diamond-like star-shaped bulbs hung everywhere, roped across the road in high-up horizontal zig-zag lines, echoed over and over again as a motif right up through the generous curve of Regent Street.

The main lights were angels, huge-winged, gracious, sparkling.

Utterly gorgeous.

There were maybe a hundred of these electric celestial creations, imparting glory over the town's busiest shopping street.

It was unlike anything which Posie – or London – had ever seen before.

Bright lights lit up Piccadilly, too, the main street running on towards Fortnum's, Green Park and The Ritz. A huge Christmas tree in a corner of Piccadilly Circus was suddenly decked out in a light-show of glory.

It was quite something to behold.

And Valentino, turning, smiling, the job done, had sauntered towards the police cordon and was signing scraps of paper which women were hurriedly placing in front of him, and he did it all with a good grace, ever the movie star.

The newspaper photographers were back, snapping all of this. Now Nita Naldi, too, was at Valentino's side, coquettish red grin in place. Snow falling on this perfectly commercial pair.

Posie felt thankful.

After all that, after those two awful notes, nothing had happened.

The Mayor and his wife were laughing, still standing at the Eros statue, shivering, but happy that the thing had gone off so well.

Posie saw Donald Derekson and Reed Amory talking together, checking Derekson's watch. Derekson's face was almost blue with the cold, and he pulled up his red scarf higher. He was stamping in the snow for a little extra warmth too, chatting with Oats, signalling things should be wrapped up. The Mayor had got his money's worth. *Time to head off.*

Somewhere from the direction of St James's Posie suddenly spied a big, burly man in his fifties, all stomach and shoulders, bull-like, come charging through the snow. He was wearing a black felt hat and an incredibly loud pin-striped suit beneath an ostentatious black fur coat, a cigar clamped in his mouth, and he was clutching some papers.

The man looked at once familiar to Posie but she couldn't place him immediately. He was fighting his way through the police cordon on that side of the Eros statue. He was shouting, bright red in the face. Posie heard the words '*CON-ARTIST!*' and something which sounded like '*wretched girl!*'

She watched as the man started to gesticulate wildly at what was going on with Valentino and the newspaper photographers. But the bobbies were having none of it, and managed to keep him back.

Posie could hear Oats' voice, ringing out through the

snow with its faintly nasal tone: 'All right, lads. That's it now! Wrap it up. Show's over. Cameras away, now. You scamper off back to your horrid little dens and make tomorrow's news for us, eh? Mr Valentino has finished up here now. Mr Valentino, would you care to come this way? And you too, Miss Naldi? I believe there is a car waiting. Where is Mrs Valentino, and Mr Amory? Ah, there.'

Reed Amory was walking right past Posie and Richard, in the direction of the lit-up Christmas tree in the corner, with Natacha Valentino at his side. He was shaking snowflakes from his smart black coat sleeves and smiling broadly, as well he should. A job well done.

Posie felt like grinning, too. 'Dolly, I do believe we are home and dry. Are you coming home with us, for some tea? Or do you fancy something at the Trocadero?'

But before Dolly Cardigeon could reply, suddenly things changed.

A whizzing noise came slicing through the air, through the snow-deadened shouts of the crowd.

Shots.

Tack–tack–tack.

It was as if the very London air crackled with the electricity it was conducting, froze itself in fear, recognised that, after all, things were not quite right here.

There were screams close by.

A man screaming, over and over.

Richard's voice came authoritatively in her ear, calm but gripped with fear: 'Posie, get down, get down on the floor. *Now.*'

Lovelace was grabbing at her, and Dolly too, and here too was Natacha Valentino, both she and Dolly like two white furry seals slipping around clumsily on the ice-packed snowy floor of the traffic island.

Reed Amory was on the floor too. 'Say, what on earth is happening? Where is Mr Valentino?'

'Get down, Mr Amory,' snapped Lovelace. 'Valentino is covered.'

Posie crouched down, careful of her belly.

Lovelace was shouting clear instructions: 'EVERYONE! Down! Head's down. Someone here has a gun! Oats, get Mr Valentino down on the floor, for the love of God. You too, man!'

There was muffled screaming from the crowds beyond, and Posie hoped beyond hope that the cordons of policemen had got the message through.

She wondered briefly if the gunman was the man in the loud pin-striped suit, if he had broken through?

Suddenly she remembered Mr Amory describing a man in a pin-striped suit hanging around at the Ritz, as if waiting for Valentino, but he had dismissed him as being not dangerous. What if Amory had been wrong and this man was now back with a more definite, dangerous game-plan?

But before she could alert Richard, there was another, closer *tack-tack-tack* sound, very close by, and Posie knew it was bullets ringing out again.

Right next to her.

She sensed sudden urgent movement, footsteps on the snow beside her, crunching. An icy hand of dreadful fear clutched at her throat, and in her belly she felt one sudden, hard kick.

It will be fine.

A staccato volley of shots.

In her fear, she panted, willing herself to breathe normally, staring at the icy, snowy London tarmac beneath her.

A dragging sound, a muffled yelp. A half scream.

There was a cracking of ice, something heavy hitting the ground beside her. A bloom of scarlet spreading on the ice.

The tang of blood.

Posie saw a red scarf trailing beside her, exposed pink florid skin. She looked up in horror, her heart pounding.

It was the Manager, Donald Derekson.

Her medical training from working on the ambulances in the Great War, never really forgotten, kicked in.

Could she help?

But no.

Help was too late for Donald Derekson now; it was too late for anything, as his lifeless brown eyes stared up forever into the never-ending snowy London night.

Posie automatically put her hand tentatively out the other way, feeling for the soft fur of Dolly's coat.

Yes, there she was. Posie breathed in relief.

It was suddenly all very quiet, quiet except for the throb of a motor nearby, and the desperate clicking, grating sound of gears being changed in a frantic hurry.

Posie looked up quickly, still on all-fours, and saw Richard was slowly getting up too, looking about for the noise of the motor-car, frowning.

'You're fine, darling girl?'

'Absolutely.'

'Good. Valentino's fine, too. Oats has done us proud.'

'And Natacha? Natacha Valentino? Where is she?'

But before Richard could answer, Fox was screaming at him.

'Look over there, sir!' Fox was yelling hoarsely, getting up off the floor, pointing through the snow.

Everything suddenly clicked into place.

'Oh, I've been a *fool*!'

Posie cursed under her breath.

'This *is* an inside job, Richard. But there's an accomplice we didn't know about. Oh, how clever. The Christmas tree! See the Christmas tree on the corner, all lit up? The motor-car is hidden behind it.'

And they looked together at the huge brightly-lit spruce in the dark corner and behind it, the shape of a dark green motor. It was trying to move off jerkily, as if the person driving it was unused to the machine. It hurtled out into the road now, spinning and skittering on the ice.

There was a flash of black-sleeved arms at the back window of the car, a press of white fur, a brief glimpse of a blurred, gagged face beneath a white cap, eyes black with kohl and terror.

'Richard! Oh, it's clever. It's a *kidnap plot*. They've got Natacha Valentino! It wasn't that she was going to go up in an actual blaze of fire, or light, but that she'd be caught up in a blaze. A blaze of *publicity!*'

'Who? What?'

They were all now on their feet, and Fox and Smallbone were running madly for the car, its wheels still spinning.

'It's the Personal Secretary, Reed Amory! He's in the back of the car, look! There's a gun pointing out the window and he's holding it! Somehow, he's connected to that girl in the café just now, the Proprietress; the one in the big paper cap. I heard Reed Amory telling the woman there was to be no hanging around. And I think he was telling her that she should be ready to drive ten minutes after the ceremony had started. His girl accomplice was the getaway driver, ready to go. It's perfect: because of the shooting, everyone is down on the ground, and the roads are completely empty. They can get away easily. The plan was always to take Natacha, and seek a ransom from Valentino.'

Fox and Smallbone were hurling themselves now at the car which was trying to get on to Piccadilly itself.

They were signalling to other policemen to break ranks and join them, but another volley of shots rang out from the car itself and the men threw themselves on the ground again.

'*STOP!*'

Suddenly the driver seemed to have got the hang of the thing at last, and the motor picked up speed and went skidding off icily down Piccadilly.

But not before Posie had seen exactly who was at the steering wheel.

A golden head, a sullen mouth, a fox-faced slip of a girl. A girl who had been acting wonderfully as the Proprietress of the café just now, and who had, earlier, been busily sashaying down the catwalk at Liberty.

The puzzle pieces came together.

Posie breathed in the icy air, a sharp sudden rush of it clearing her mind.

Richard was marching about, giving quick, angry orders. For a few minutes Posie saw him engaged in a heated conversation with the furious, red-faced man in the pin-striped suit who simply wouldn't go away.

Oh, of course.

Sure as bread was bread the angry man in the pin-striped suit was the same one she had seen at Liberty, earlier. In the row of deckchairs, smoking, alone, and again slightly later on the arm of the sullen-faced blonde model as they moved down the stairs together, as she passed him paperwork.

Hadn't he been clutching at paperwork just a few minutes ago? What was all that about?

And was he in on the kidnap plot? Somehow he was linked to the sulky-faced model, of that Posie was sure.

Posie watched as the big man was handed over to a bobby who got out a notebook, writing things down furiously in it. The bobby was staring in incomprehension at the big man's paperwork which had been shoved under his nose.

But the big man seemed appeased, at least; was lighting up another smoke, not shouting or charging at anyone anymore.

Oats was the most scared Posie had ever seen him, and was now bundling his charges towards the shelter of the café from which they had come, the Mayor and Mayoress following, wide-eyed and alarmed.

Fox and Smallbone were barking instructions to the ranks of policemen, telling the crowds to get off home. There was nothing to be seen here anymore.

Well, that much was true.

Richard had thrown his own overcoat over the body of Donald Derekson and the flash-lights of cameramen could get nothing more revealing than a picture of a good, dark Harris Tweed and a smidgen of red scarf sticking out.

Posie saw a small, white fluffy figure still sitting crouched on the snowy floor, arms wrapped tightly around her knees.

'Dolly, darling. Are you okay? Get up, you'll catch your death down there. And Rufus will kill me.'

She bent down to pull her friend up, yanked at her hand, but then she got the shock of her life.

For the figure suddenly looked up from beneath the white turban glittering with sequins, and it wasn't Dolly at all.

It was Natacha Valentino sitting there, and tears were coursing down her face.

****

Seven

It was a scene of utter madness, forever to be remembered, but best forgotten.

Crowds slowly retreating into the night, down into Underground stations, off in big groups up the still traffic-free streets. Snow continuing to fall.

Posie was tugging at Richard's thin jacket sleeve. She saw he was shivering without his coat. 'They've got Dolly,' she said as calmly as was possible.

'*What?*'

'There's been a frightful mix-up. They were obviously going to take Natacha Valentino, but they've got Dolly instead: from the back, lying on the ground, the two women were pretty near identical. I reckon Reed Amory in his haste grabbed at the wrong woman and bundled her into the car, and they had set off before they realised their mistake. They're probably only realising it now.'

'Oh, by Jove! If they realise they have the wrong woman…no, it doesn't bear thinking about. Oh, golly! They're heartless scoundrels willing to risk murder in cold blood in a big public open space, so what will they do to Dolly? They have a gun! Or guns, I expect.'

Lovelace had turned absolutely white, his lips blue, and if he had been a more religious man Posie thought he would have crossed himself about now.

For herself, panic and desperation had been ousted quickly, and all Posie could think about was getting her friend home safely.

'Maybe they will notice the quality of her clothes, the real diamonds she's wearing? And then they will understand they have someone on their hands whom they can use in the same way as Natacha Valentino? Maybe they will blackmail Rufus? It's the best we can hope for.'

Lovelace groaned: 'If only we knew who they *were*. Where they're heading in that car. Driving out of Piccadilly probably means they're heading for open country, eventually.'

But Posie, with that clear-headed determination which was so necessary now, shook her head. 'Don't criminals usually go *home*? Back to where they are from? It's a sort of basic, homing instinct.'

'And? We don't know where "home" is for them, do we, love?'

Posie bit her lip, licked away the last remnants of her pink Maybelline lipstick.

'Perhaps we do. Reed Amory is American, or else very good at *playing* an American. He's only been with Valentino for a few months, since just before they left America for Europe. What if he joined Valentino exactly for *this*, for this plan to work? We don't know anything about him except he has a girlfriend called Henrietta. I *supposed* she was an American; I know he was calling her from the Café de Paris, but what if it was simply a local number he asked for? Maybe the call was only being put through to here in Piccadilly? To this local café which the mysterious Henrietta had managed to pose as the Proprietress of? What if she's a local girl? What if they are *both* local? Sam Stubbs said the woman who called him had a very strong East End accent. As did the other newspaper editors.'

She was suddenly remembering the model elbowing her way into the telephone booth at Liberty after the show, at three-thirty. 'Yes. I'm pretty sure it was *her* calling those newspapers, you know. The timing fits, even if I don't know why she did it, exactly.'

Richard Lovelace looked as if he had just swallowed a very bitter pill indeed.

Natacha Valentino was still sitting on the floor, shivering. Lovelace helped her up and walked the girl to the café. He opened the glass door, practically thrusting the girl inside.

She ran to Valentino's arms and started crying hysterically.

The Mayor's wife was pouring everyone coffee from a big serving-urn set up on the back counter, Nita Naldi carrying mugs about, ashen-faced. Oats was gulping at his drink almost automatically, his eyes rather wild.

But Lovelace wasn't done. 'Oats,' he commanded. 'Here, *now*. You've not done anything wrong, man, and I daresay there's a bravery award in this mess for you tonight; probably the highest you can get. But I need your help *now*.'

On the entrance mat they stood, the three of them, looking out towards the tweed-covered body of Donald Derekson, now covered in a blanket of snow.

'Chief Commissioner?'

'"*Henrietta*." I'm just speaking aloud that name. Ring any bells with you? It does with me, but I must confess I think I've seen it on a case-file and put it to the back of my mind. I can't place it. East End girl…'

Posie chipped in with what she knew. 'Long-limbed, tall girl. Golden hair, very fashionable. Pretty until you see her face. I think she was working as a model today at Liberty, and then she was working here, dressed all in black with a white paper hat, just before the lights ceremony. She was also driving that getaway car.'

Oats had gripped his tatty moustache, his blue eyes bulging with excitement and trepidation. This was a turning point – a crucial pivot – in his whole career. You could just tell.

'Henrietta? Oh, yes, Miss Parker. I know exactly who you mean. Henrietta Styles. She's known as "Chicky" Styles to all and sundry in the criminal underworld of London.'

Oats was slowly joining the dots. 'You mean, that was *her*?' He cursed under his breath. 'I thought there was something about her which looked familiar when we were in here earlier.'

Posie shrugged. 'What's this Chicky like? And more importantly, where does she live?'

Oats was turning amazed eyes from Posie to Richard, looking askance. 'She's been removed from our "Most Wanted" list of criminals these last few months; we reckoned she'd been lying low for some reason. Before that, take your pick as to what she's like. One of the best professional gambling crooks in London. Pretty darn good at scrubbing up well, and can change her appearance quicker than you can say "knife". Over the last couple of years she's been getting jobs as a croupier in different gambling dens and casinos, adding a touch of glamour to these places. She plays it straight for a while, then she usually skews the gambling odds and takes home the bacon.'

'Gambling odds, eh?' Lovelace raised an eyebrow, interested. 'Hmnn…'

'She's guilty of other stuff, too, sir: petty violence, theft, robbery, jewels going missing.'

'Any *actual* violence, Oats?'

'Nah. Not like the gang she hangs with. Now *they're* a proper horrible bunch. Based over by London Bridge, they are. Chicky had a lad there. Nasty piece of work, he was. Famous. But we'd given up the scent on him, too, these last few months. We hoped he'd done a bunk. Further away the better for us, we all reckoned. Off our patch with any luck. We thought he'd moved Stateside maybe, or Australia.'

Oh, he went. But he came back.

Came back with a plan.

Posie took a deep breath before she asked: 'What was Chicky's lads' name? And what did he look like?'

Oats drew himself up his full height, confident now in his knowledge.

'Tommy Doolley is the name of the lad in question, and he's a career criminal. He's been raised as a criminal and he's stayed one. He's one of the best shots in London, and into everything unpalatable. Good-looking boy, though. Very handsome. Butter wouldn't melt, some might say. Scrubbed up well on occasion, too. He could even play the toff, with the nice accent to boot. Which is how he managed to get into all the places he did. You remember the affair of the Atterley rubies? The mysterious George Sinclair?'

Posie nodded, and Lovelace groaned, covering his face.

Six months back Lady Stephania Atterley, a debutante, had scandalised society by stepping out with a virtual unknown on several occasions in town. The unknown had been a lovely-looking dark boy called George Sinclair, whose easy-on-the-eye appearance had often been captured for the newspapers, laughing and smiling with Stephania on his arm.

George Sinclair had disappeared one night, along with Stephania's priceless jewels. Never to be seen again. Stephania had been found in a hotel room, trussed up like a turkey but mercifully otherwise unhurt, and had kept out of the spotlight ever since. But the reputation, and the finances, of the Atterley family had never recovered.

Posie was staggered. '*That* was Tommy Doolley? *He* was George Sinclair?'

'Yes. But we managed to keep it all hush-hush. Doolley went to ground, disappeared.'

Posie nodded. 'Seems his girlfriend Chicky and he share a knack of being able to pull off disguises.'

Oats stiffened. 'You mean…'

'Yes. That suntanned, white-toothed athlete of an American lad was Tommy Doolley. Busy with the disguises again. I'm sure of it. Only now everything's gone wrong. Let's hope he treats Dolly with as much mercy as poor Stephania Atterley. And not like he did with that poor Manager over there. For I'm sure it was Tommy Doolley with the gun, aren't you, Richard?'

'Absolutely. It was jolly clever. A few shots into the air when he was walking, then, when he was down, in all the chaos, a few shots again at close range. Dangerous devil. Let's hope he treats the Countess well.'

Oats was only just cottoning on to how things stood: 'Sorry? What? You mean? The Countess has been…'

'Kidnapped. Yes,' answered Posie as calmly as she could.

But Lovelace was being more practical. He'd pulled out the waxed and folded map of the whole of London he always carried in his inside jacket pocket.

He was standing over it, jabbing.

'London Bridge, eh? We may be in bally luck. They'll do a big loop past Buckingham Palace, trying to drive through the city and on to the Embankment, but they'll run into trouble at the Palace itself, coming up into Victoria. The traffic wasn't stopped there: and it's crazy this time of the evening, with lots of buses in queues, on diversion from here. I'll bet my coat out there in the snow that if we get in a police-car and head to that snarled-up traffic scene, we'll be able to pluck the Countess out from their car in one piece. And we'll arrest Doolley and Styles to boot. I'll not let them get away with this. It's a scandal! We need armed men, but I hope not to have to resort to guns. It would be good to rely on the element of surprise.'

He dragged his hands through his hair, annoyed at himself. 'Dash it all, I *thought* there was something familiar about the lad when I spied him earlier at the Café de Paris, but the lights, the music, the movie stars, it was all too much for me.'

'I was taken in too, Chief Commissioner. Good and proper. You want me to come with you, Guv?'

'No, I'll take Fox. You get all these good people to a place of safety. The Americans are staying at The Ritz, so straight back there would be good.'

'On it, sir.'

Posie glanced over at the Americans, and she suddenly caught Rudolph Valentino's eye. He gave a despairing kind of shrug in her direction, a strained smile which seemed to refer to Natacha's safe passage, and he mouthed '*Thank you.*'

Posie nodded, thoughts racing.

I didn't do anything: it was all a mess. But at least you are alive, and your wife is, too. And Nita Naldi.

But Dolly…

As if he could read her mind, Valentino mouthed: '*I'm so sorry.*'

The film star looked as if he was about to hurry over to Posie, when he suddenly saw someone at the door, and froze.

Posie turned and, sure enough, a familiar man was at the glass door, pushing it open. A welcome one. It was Sam Stubbs, Editor of the *Associated Press*, grown fatter and balder since Posie had seen him last, enviably well-wrapped up in a good thick coat of serge wool.

'What-ho! What an evening!'

Sam Stubbs suddenly saw the movie stars inside the café, huddled near the counter, grim-faced, holding their coffees as if their lives depended on it, somehow penned in, and his eyes widened like saucers.

'I say! Any chance of an exclusive?'

'Not on your nelly,' said Lovelace smartly, 'but give me your coat, and take Posie here somewhere safe and unknown for something hot to eat and we'll see what we can do by way of an exclusive in the morning. You know a good place, right?'

****

Eight

It was seven-thirty.

Posie sat at a red plush-velvet banquette in a grotty tiny café tucked behind the Burlington Arcade, near the Albany.

This was Kitty's. It was the sort of place which catered for fading actresses and down-at-heel generals and the like, and Sam Stubbs obviously knew it well. He made a habit, in fact, of knowing and using the smallest, dingiest cafés across town, and was a regular in many.

This café served three things: coffee; ham, egg and chips; and coconut macaroons. Posie had had plenty of the first two, and was now attacking the third, final offering.

At the banquette sat Dolly, all a-jitter with the tale of her evening, together with Lovelace, Sergeant Fox and Constable Smallbone, and Sam Stubbs, who was open-mouthed, notebook on table, pencil in hand.

Oats was also there, munching on a bowl of chips with plenty of salt sprinkled on top.

Ten minutes earlier Lovelace had burst through the curtain-covered door of Kitty's, with Dolly right behind him, his men beside her, looking relieved and exultant.

They'd managed to infiltrate the green getaway car, just past Victoria, stuck, as predicted, in a traffic jam. They'd dragged out a bound-and-gagged Dolly, who had promptly fallen out of the car seat straight into a water-filled slushy pothole, but, other than that, she was fine.

They'd also managed to arrest her captors without recourse to using arms.

And now for reflections.

Honesty.

Understanding it all.

'So, Tommy Doolley masterminded the whole thing, didn't he?' asked Posie of her husband.

'Probably got wind of the fact that this ill-fated shopping spree to Europe was in the offing and attached himself to Rudolph Valentino specifically, to bring off a kidnapping wheeze like this. On his home-turf. That's right, isn't it?'

'Exactly,' said Richard, handing back Sam Stubbs's jolly nice coat, and shaking out a cigarette from his battered tin. He lit up his Murad and inhaled the smoke with enjoyment.

Lovelace continued: 'He was good at playing his part; that of a smart young American from a good, established family in The Hamptons. It was clever. You see, Valentino and Nita Naldi and even Natacha Valentino are exactly the kind of people whose eyes you could pull the wool over. Valentino is an immigrant Italian, and both Miss Naldi and Mrs Valentino are from immigrant Irish families. So Doolley, as Reed Amory, was quite the genuine settled American article to them. A study of manners and sophistication, and a good employee as well: organised; amiable; clever. Valentino and his wife were mainly focused on the Paris trip. I reckon it was Tommy Doolley who suggested this quick and easy jaunt to London and he would have organised all the hotel and aeroplane bookings, probably paying with Valentino's cheque book.'

'I think that's right,' agreed Posie. 'I know he was in charge of booking and arranging flights. But what about Donald Derekson?' asked Posie, confused. 'Where did *he* fit in?'

'I'm not a hundred per cent sure,' said Lovelace, shaking off the ash. 'We'll question Tommy Doolley in the morning, or else Miss Styles, if her gentleman friend isn't up for talking. When they've had a night in our nice cold cells to mull things over, maybe they'll come to view cooperation as the best approach. Meanwhile, they can stew on the mess they're actually in.'

Posie continued: 'But it was Derekson who did the actual booking with the Mayor for the appearance tonight, so he was obviously "in" on something, wasn't he? Even if it was just pocketing that big fat fee?'

'That sounds about right,' said Oats, rolling his eyes, crunching on a chip.

Lovelace shrugged: 'I reckon Doolley suggested the event to Derekson; sold it to him as a quick way of making money, but no doubt it was Doolley's little brainchild. But was Derekson's death an accident?' mulled Lovelace, stubbing out his smoke and pouring himself coffee from the pot on the table. 'I wonder if Derekson had rumbled Dooley?'

Dolly, who was also drinking hot coffee, and seemed completely unperturbed by her experience, trilled excitedly:

'I was listenin' to them as we drove along, before they discovered I wasn't who I was supposed to be! It *was* him who killed the Manager, for sure. It was no accident! The girl drivin' was furious. She kept saying: "*This has all gone wrong! So wrong! We weren't goin' to kill anyone!*" And he had the devil of a temper on him, that pretty boy with his fake bronze tan. He was shoutin', too. Saying, "*I had to, Chicky. He'd found out about Raddisons. He wanted a cut of it. I couldn't let that happen. I think he had a fair clue as to what I was up to with the kidnap plans, too. He'd made a few odd remarks about how he wished a kidnapper would come along and save us all a lot of trouble, but it was with a laugh and a knowing look. Nah, it was too risky lettin' him live…*"'

Posie frowned, something was unclear. She'd never understood betting terms, or practices. 'Raddisons?'

She turned to Smallbone, and then to Sam Stubbs. 'Didn't one of you mention Raddisons in Covent Garden were offering crazily remote odds on Rudolph Valentino being the mystery guest to turn on the Christmas lights tonight?'

Both men nodded.

Sam Stubbs checked his own notebook. 'It was 500/1. Virtually impossible odds. The bookie must have had some knowledge that Valentino was going to be in town today: they don't like to let odds be placed on imaginary happenings, but also, they must have been fairly certain, watertight, in fact, that Valentino *wasn't* going to be the one to turn the lights on. To offer odds like that. If you'd betted big in Valentino's favour, you'd have cleaned them out. As I expect a fair few men have.'

'That's what this fella was goin' to do!' said Dolly, excitedly. 'He had some third party from his home turf who had placed the bet, and was goin' to go around in the mornin' and pick up his winnings. He kept mentioning a fella called Hamish. Hamish McBride.'

Oats and Lovelace locked eyes and raised eyebrows. Obviously that name meant something to them. Something bad.

Lovelace crossed his arms. 'Whatever happened, our Mr Raddison realised he had been played for a fool. He came up here in person tonight, to the ceremony, as angry as I think I've ever seen a man. Demanding to speak to anyone in charge, to Valentino himself, if necessary.'

That made sense. Posie nodded. 'The man in the navy pin-striped suit? Big fella? Cigar? *That* was Mr Raddison?'

'That's the one.' Lovelace grinned slightly wolfishly. 'You know him, darling?'

'Hardly. But I saw him earlier this afternoon, at the Grand Opening at Liberty, at a fashion show which couldn't have interested him in a million years. He was sitting next to Valentino and Natacha, as if checking they were really there. He looked pretty convinced. Happy. The girl, Chicky Styles, obviously got herself hired there as a model to get access to the very exclusive show, and called Mr Raddison beforehand, asking him to attend, promising him 'exclusive' information. He wasn't to know she was dancing to Tommy Doolley's tune, was he? That the whole thing was a professionally-run criminal set-up?'

Richard Lovelace raised an eyebrow incredulously. '*That* will be why Raddison offered the odds, then. But he must have thought it hugely unlikely Valentino would be here tonight, switching the lights on. So what made him think that?'

'When were they supposed to be leaving?' cut in Fox, frowning.

'They were supposed to be flying back to Paris tomorrow night,' answered Posie.

And then she was suddenly remembering the staircase at Liberty, the model passing a piece of paper to Raddison.

'Oh! Oh! I see! What if this girl, Chicky Styles, promised she would show Raddison fool-proof evidence that Valentino would be out of London tonight? Gone. All she would need to do would be to obtain the real, authentic flying papers from Tommy Doolley.'

'But you said they were flying *tomorrow*, Miss,' said Smallbone, frowning.

'That's what Tommy Doolley told Valentino and the group, and they trusted his 'organisation'. What if Tommy had actually booked return flights for *tonight*? On purpose? And these were the papers Chicky showed Raddison at Liberty, with today's date on them? This would have been solid evidence that Valentino wasn't planning on being in town tonight. Chicky could have pretended to have a fancy-man at Croydon Aerodrome who'd given her the papers, or something like that. Could have said she thought it might be interesting to Raddison, as she'd heard other bookies were taking bets on which famous guest might turn the lights on, and were cleaning up: maybe Raddison could get in on the action too? Maybe she told him the newspapers would be full of speculation about it tonight. And she'd have known: she was the informant! I expect she asked Raddison for some pathetically-small retainer for her assistance in the thing, and because of that Raddison marked her down as some small-fry chancer! And all of this cleverly-planned staging led Raddison to open up the betting on Valentino. Talk about neat!'

Lovelace was nodding. 'Sounds about right.'

Posie went on: 'Nita Naldi overheard Tommy Doolley on the telephone to Croydon Aerodrome this afternoon, buying more tickets. Those were probably for flights tomorrow, and they would be couriered to the hotel. So no one would ever have been the wiser: Valentino definitely wouldn't have noticed he'd paid for the flights twice, on two subsequent days, and Doolley would be home and dry. Although by the time the party came to be flying back to Paris, he planned to have vanished, taking Natacha Valentino with him. And having cleaned Raddisons out, to boot.'

Posie turned to her husband. 'Have you looked at the papers which Raddison was brandishing tonight, darling? The ones the bobby on the street was reading?'

Lovelace shook his head. 'Not yet. They'll be on file at Scotland Yard though by now. Why?'

'I'd get someone to check them out. I'm sure you'll find they are the aeroplane tickets with todays' date on them.'

Lovelace grinned. 'Attagirl, darling! Fox, check it out after this. We'll need every bit of physical, real evidence we can muster when we interview Doolley in the morning.'

Fox frowned. 'Of course. And we think Donald Derekson got wind of this nice arrangement and demanded his share of the Raddisons winnings?'

'Oh, yes!' Dolly nodded, stuffing a rock-hard coconut macaroon in her mouth as she did so.

Lovelace bit at his lip. 'Seems odd that Derekson would have let a kidnap happen, though, doesn't it? It was to no one's benefit.'

Posie disagreed. 'It was, though. Natacha and her new film and everything she represented were dreadful to him and his film company, Ariad. He told me he wished Valentino would get together with Nita Naldi for real. If Natacha died, it was no loss to him. And if she lived, maybe she'd have been so cowed she wouldn't have interfered in her husband's films again.'

Fox had hardly eaten a thing, nor touched the coffee. He smoked now, seriously. 'Those notes you showed us earlier, sir. The threats sent to Valentino? I'm confused. Who wrote them?'

Lovelace had brought the very things out from his pocket and placed them on the table, smoothed them out. But Posie got in first.

'It was Reed Amory's work, or Tommy Doolley, as we now know him as. He was a man who wasn't afraid of being blatant, taking risks. He was utterly convincing. He telephoned Chicky Styles from The Ritz reception, pretending to talk to the Mayor's Office: giving her timings about tonight. All of this with Nita Naldi and the Manager, Donald Derekson, sitting nearby!'

Oats was shaking his head. 'But these notes actively suggest a *threat*, and I reckon any normal famous person would run for the hills if faced with this kind of thing. What the deuce did Tommy Doolley think he was doing?'

But Posie understood, because she had spent those precious moments with 'The Sheik' himself.

'I think Tommy Doolley really got the measure of Valentino. He understood him well, realised he was sort of naïve. It was as if Valentino couldn't believe that bad things would happen to him; treated things as a laugh. Nita Naldi described him as "trusting". The threats contained such detailed information that they *had* to be from someone in

Rudolph Valentino's inside circle, and he couldn't believe that one of those people would hurt either him or his wife. This bizarre trust meant he would never – not for a minute – think of not appearing at a scheduled event. He was professional, and he had been led to believe it was a favour he was bestowing on the town, so he wouldn't let people down. He laughed when I suggested it might actually be dangerous. So Dooley relied on this trust, and knew that rather than putting Valentino off, the threats would rather *ensure* his attendance.'

Fox nodded slowly. He was very into theories. 'A kind of reverse psychology then?'

'Pah! Reverse something or other!' muttered Oats impatiently.

Posie shrugged. 'The threats were clever, as they could later be used by the police 'against' Valentino: you lot could say he'd been warned about trouble for his wife, after all. Perhaps Doolley was hoping someone else might take the rap for the whole mess, too: once he'd disappeared, an investigation might take in Donald Derekson as having been partly to blame, or -and this was clever- maybe even Mr Raddison himself. Tommy Doolley had already thrown me fake evidence as to having seen a man of Raddison's exact appearance hanging around the Ritz and acting suspiciously earlier today, the same time the second note was supposedly delivered for Valentino.'

'Pah! It's a mare's nest, and no mistake,' offered Oats, clamping on his hat. He looked grimly satisfied: 'He'll hang of course, Doolley, for this murder. And good riddance to bad rubbish!'

'I wouldn't count on it, Bill.' Lovelace sighed. 'He can plead manslaughter if he gets a good brief, which he will. And then it's just a jail term. We'll bring charges of corruption on Raddison's behalf; mis-appropriated evidence under 'The Gambling Act', of course. And fixing the outcome of a commercial bet. But that's just a jail term, too.'

Chief Inspector Oats sighed heavily, and nodded goodbye. He was making for The Ritz, where he was personally charged with sitting outside the doors to the Valentino's suite, and Nita Naldi's next door. Tomorrow he would escort them with a police guard to Croydon Aerodrome, for their return flight to Paris.

'I wonder if they'll ever return to London,' mused Posie, leaning back tiredly. Outside the snow seemed to be even heavier.

'Bound to, Miss Parker,' said Sam Stubbs, putting his notebook away. 'This is the best city in the world. Even with gun-toting maniacs on the loose! Not a moment goes by without some excitement, eh?'

Coats and hats were being put on, Fox and Smallbone returning to New Scotland Yard.

'I'm going to get a motor-taxi,' said Lovelace to Dolly. 'Get Posie home, and I'll turn in, too. She's tired and I'm freezing. You want to come along or are you heading home to Chelsea? Are you sure you're fine, Lady Cardigeon? After your ordeal_ I must confess I was scared witless on your behalf. You can't think how relieved I was to get you out of that car.'

Dolly grinned and there was a mad sparkle in her eye.

'Don't you worry about me, Richard. I've never been better. And I don't want to go home now, do I? Not when there's somethin' life-changing about to happen. Somethin' new in London. Happenin' tonight! An exclusive.'

Sam Stubbs looked up immediately at the word 'exclusive'.

'What is it, Lady Cardigeon? Can I come along?'

Dolly shrugged. She was putting on that priceless white coat again, but it was marked and grubby now, as if she had fallen in a muddy puddle, which, in effect, she had.

'Don't see why not, Sam. But you'll need to be able to move. Dance like you've never danced before. Have you heard of the Charleston? No? You should have. It's taken

America by storm. Your readers will want to hear all about this. There's this little slip of a thing, she's called Louise Brooks…'

And with that exchange, Dolly and Sam Stubbs had disappeared.

Posie and Richard stepped out into the snow, hailed a motor-cab opposite Fortnum's.

As they swung through a now congested Piccadilly Circus, they looked up Regent Street at the angels in all their bold electric glory. Richard, still without a coat, took Posie's hand.

'They're quite beautiful really, aren't they, the lights?' he said, earnestly.

'Absolutely, I'm sure they will become iconic.' Posie smiled happily. 'And I agree with Sam; it really is the best city in the world. It's dressed up like a Duchess in all these lights tonight and it looks fantastic, but by day it's pretty lovely too.'

'Just like you, Posie.'

She laughed at the compliment.

She had picked up her small Christmas tree favour again, turned on the blinking tiny lights inside it.

'I think I'm going to throw this away when we get home. I can't chance this going up in flames. Like poor Natacha Valentino's did. What a horrid coincidence. I actually felt rather sorry for the girl. I *do* feel sorry for her. I can't think her film will go well after all this, can you?'

Lovelace stayed with the here-and-now. 'Who knows, darling? And yes, I agree about that little toy. Dangerous. It's much the best thing to throw it away.'

'I'm glad *you're* not a movie star, Richard. What a funny old life! Valentino was adorable, but life for him is so complicated.'

And all the way up to Museum Chambers in Bloomsbury, as London passed by outside, Posie felt a flurry of several small kicks inside.

It wasn't just Louise Brooks who was making history tonight.

Someone brand new on the scene was taking the opportunity to dance a wonderful new dance.

* * * *

Wartime, RAF Detling, 1944
(Twenty years later)

Epilogue

Phyllis Lovelace was known as the most sensible of girls in the Headquarters where they were barracked. She was Head Officer, after all.

She wasn't given to fancy, or to romance.

She was probably the only girl in the whole unit of girl Royal Air Force Officials who hadn't moaned as supplies of lipstick and nylon stockings had gone from running low to being absolutely non-existent.

On the small bedside table next to her immaculate single bed were only ever two items.

One was a cheap pink necklace of Murano glass beads, given to her by her mother when she'd first been sent here. For luck.

The second was a framed black and white photograph. It showed a beautiful dark young man, jauntily plucking at the lapels of his fashionable summer suit, an expensive cigar clamped in his lips, leaning nonchalantly against a wall. Impossibly gorgeous. The photograph was from a movie called *Blood and Sand*, and it had been taken when Phyllis herself was only about one year old.

She'd never met the man in the photograph, as he had died, tragically young, in 1926, when she was just five years old, and he was thirty-one years old.

And yet the photograph bore an inscription just for her, the writing slanting upwards, the signature exaggerated and curving.

For little Phyllis,
Thank you for loaning me your mommy and daddy last night, they sure helped me out.
Yours in gratitude,
Rudolph Valentino

It had passed into family folklore how Valentino had come to Posie's office on Grape Street in Bloomsbury the day after the incident of the murder in the London lights, with flowers and a sincere offer to take Posie out for lunch.

But Posie Parker hadn't been in: she'd been at a hospital appointment at Great Ormond Street nearby, and while Valentino had waited, the appointment had dragged on, and he'd had to go.

He had left the signed photograph and the flowers on Posie's desk, leaving a completely speechless Sidney, the Office Boy, and Prudence, the Secretary, in his wake.

This almost-lunch with Rudolph Valentino was always trotted out at Lovelace family gatherings over the years, with Posie still regretful, sentimental almost, at the missed opportunity.

Phyllis grinned now.

She was brushing her thick brown hair up into the flouncy chignon which all the girls wore, jamming on her blue WAAF hat, ready for an early breakfast.

A new girl had been given the bed next to hers and she was nervous, trying to make conversation.

'Who's that, then?' the new girl said, pointing at the photograph. She looked from Phyllis, who was not a beauty, to the photograph and back again, slightly rudely. 'He's not your fella, is he?'

'Gosh, no. I don't have a fella. But he's a little bit of sparkle, right enough. A symbol, if you like.'

'Oh? What of?'

'Light,' said Phyllis, certainly, standing up, smoothing down her navy serge dress-jacket.

'And hope. A sign that beauty and light can never really be extinguished. Even in dreadful dark times, like now, the memory of what was truly wonderful lives on.'

And then she walked out, mess-hall bound, for a cup of tea with plenty of sugar in it and a hot bacon roll.

* * * *

Historical Note

All of the characters in this book are fictional, unless specifically mentioned.

For real-life characters whom I have placed within the fictional story, see Notes 1 to 9 below.

As in the other Posie Parker books, I refer to the First World War of 1914–1918 as the 'Great War' throughout, which is simpler for the modern reader, although it would not have been referred to in this way in 1924.

As ever, both Posie's work address in London (Grape Street, Bloomsbury, WC1) and her home address around the corner (Museum Chambers, WC1) are both very real, although you might have to do a bit of imagining to find her there.

Slightly more so than with other Posie Parker novels and novellas, I have played rather hard and fast with the historical accuracy of dates here to suit my fictional storyline.

This novella takes place on 18 December, 1924.

What is absolutely unequivocally made up by me is Rudolph Valentino's turning on of the Christmas lights at Piccadilly. This did *not* happen, and could not have happened in a million years, as the Christmas lights of angels etc as we know them were only hung and lit from

1954 onwards, when local retailers paid for a display of lights in a desperate bid to show that post-war London could look wonderful, and not at all 'drab'.

It is a tradition which has continued to the present day.

It is however accurate to say that 1924 was an interesting year in London.

The Café de Paris, at 3 Coventry Street, London W1, opened up and (by the date of this novella) it was roaringly successful. A young Louise Brooks did indeed dance the Charleston here in December for the first time, introducing the dance craze to London. And favours such as I describe in this story were routinely given out.

And Liberty, the beautiful new department store just off Regent Street also opened in December 1924 (the Grand Opening and Fashion Show which I describe here is, however, a fancy all of my own).

But I have been creative with the dates around Rudolph Valentino and his entourage's presence in London.

What is certain is that the world-famous silent-movie star Rudolph Valentino and his wife, Natacha Rambova, visited London in August 1923 as part of a European tour. And that Valentino was again in London – but very much alone – from the last week of November 1925. He was staying for several months at the Hyde Park Hotel on the 1925 trip, officially publicising his latest film for United Artists, *The Eagle*, and spending money recklessly as his divorce from Natacha went through.

What is also certain is that he was also in Europe, mainly Paris, and perhaps fleetingly in London by way of Croydon Aerodrome, in 1924, when he and his wife Natacha, together with the film star Nita Naldi (his co-star from the film *Blood and Sand*, 1922, and *Cobra*, 1924) spent three months being fitted for costumes and spending frankly outrageous amounts of money on fabrics, costumes and sets and scenery for *The Hooded Falcon*. It is this real-life buying-spree which I use here as a very rough background or springboard for this fictional novella.

That Valentino and Natacha could have been interested in attending the fictional Liberty event I describe seems eminently within the realms of possibility, as the store is justly famous for its wonderful fabrics and fashion, now as then.

It is worth mentioning that in reality *The Hooded Falcon* was a film which seemed doomed to failure from the start. This was a film whose script had been penned by Natacha, with costumes designed by her, and with Valentino and Nita Naldi in the proposed starring roles. With most of the budget having been spent before filming started, the real-life Ritz-Carlton company (the company Valentino was actually signed to at this period) terminated the deal just before filming started up in Hollywood. This debacle arguably signalled the end of the Valentino's marriage, set Valentino himself on a course of financial disaster, and saw him switch contracts to become represented by Charlie Chaplin's United Artists.

In this novella I have Valentino being 'managed' and accompanied by a fictional businessman, Donald Derekson, whose company, 'Ariad Films', is bankrolling the spending-spree. This character and company are entirely fictional, as is the Personal Secretary, Reed Amory. As are all the main events of the story, which is pure fiction in itself.

I have taken a wild fancy to set Valentino among the Christmas lights and general glamour of London in December 1924, while in absolute reality he was by this time starting to film *The Eagle* back in America.

I do not believe Valentino knew Louise Brooks at this very early stage in her career (they were certainly acquainted by 1926, when she had achieved massive fame all of her own as a silver-screen star) and I do not think he had one of the very few permissions to use the secret staircase to the Café de Paris, WC1, but this is simply a story, and stories are designed for escapism.

(This is not a definitive history, for which there are some excellent biographies.)

1. Rudolph Valentino (1895–1926)

Rudolph Valentino was (and still is) arguably the most important American (Italian-American) film star of all time. His smouldering dark good looks and athleticism were a perfect and heady combination for the silent movies of the 1920s. Arguably 'peaking' early with the 1921 film, *The Sheik* (which defined his career, image and legacy), it was this film which got him the nicknames of 'The Latin Lover', or 'The Great Lover', or simply 'Valentino'. His tragically early death at the age of thirty-one perhaps intensified the interest and hysteria in Valentino, in a way which it is doubtful would have been the case if he had lived to old age, as his 'style' would probably not have survived the advent of the 'talkies'.

Desperate to escape the legacy of *The Sheik*, it is ironic that his financial difficulties towards the end of his life compelled him to accept the starring role in *The Son of The Sheik*, which was much on similar lines. Valentino was famously angry at frequent press attacks upon him as being 'effeminate' and a threat to the 'all-American' man, with talk of male cinema goers leaving theatres in disgust when his films were playing. What cannot be denied though is that most American men would have loved to look like Valentino, with his every fashion and hairstyle copied slavishly across the country.

As in this novella, he famously lived by his reviews and carried newspaper clippings both praising and critiquing his film appearances around with him everywhere.

2. Valentino's wife, Natacha Valentino (nee Rambova) (1897–1966)

Descended from Irish immigrant parents and adopting a more 'Russian' stage-name, Natacha was a controversial, tempestuous figure at the best of times. A dancer, costume designer and occasional actress, she first met Valentino on the set of *Camille* in 1921, marrying him in 1922. But even that was beset by problems, as he was already married to Jean Acker, another American film actress, and what followed was a complete farce involving fake separations, Valentino being jailed for bigamy and a remarriage in 1923. Friends of Valentino (and later his agents) feared Natacha's controlling manner and domineering personality over Valentino and her monopoly on the work he chose, attributing to her his spiralling lack of popularity during the 1920s. Indeed, Valentino's contract with United Artists in 1924 banned Natacha from producing any films he made for them, and excluded her from the film sets themselves. Valentino's acceptance of these terms marked the beginning of the end of their marriage, although it must have been in trouble for some time.

3. Nita Naldi (1894–1961)

With a very similar Irish immigrant background to Natacha Rambova (see Note 2 above), Nita Naldi became internationally famous with her role in the 1922 film *Blood and Sand*, together with Valentino. She became known as a beautiful 'vamp' and often played such characters, frequently co-starring with Valentino throughout the 1920s, and ended her career with the advent of the 'talkies'. She did indeed accompany the Valentinos on their crazily excessive trip to Europe in 1924, buying for *The Hooded Falcon*.

4. Harry Roy (1900–1971)

Aged just twenty-four when this novella is set, Harry Roy (real name Harry Lipman) was already a well-known dance-band leader and hugely talented clarinettist on the London music scene. With his brother Sidney he played in the Crichton Lyricals in a regular spot at the Café de Paris for three years, before going on to tour internationally. He became nationally famous with his big band, Harry Roy's Tiger Ragamuffins, during the Second World War, but he played right up until the 1960s.

5. Layton & Johnstone

This American vocal and piano duo worked throughout the 1920s and 1930s, moving to England in 1922 after having had enormous success in clubs across New York City. As in this novella, they had a permanent residence at the Café de Paris, and were personal favourites of the then Prince of Wales. They frequently appeared on BBC radio, selling more than ten million records across their most popular years.

6. Martin Poulson

Martin Poulson had been in charge at the London-famous Embassy Club, before being poached by the owners of the new Café de Paris, on its creation in 1924. They made him a Director. He was well-known for his discretion, and knew most of London society at the time this novella is set. He famously had the ear of the Prince of Wales and in physical looks is pretty much how I describe. I have had to invent the personality of the man.

7. Louise Brooks (1906–1985)

Before she became the jazz-age icon and world-famous actress of films such as *Pandora's Box* (1927), Louise Brooks was, from the age of fifteen, a chorus-girl and a dancer. Already sporting her famous chopped black bob, in 1924 she indeed came to London and was booked to work at the Café de Paris, dancing the Charleston there (for the first time in England) in December 1924.

8. Dolly Tree (1899-1962)

Dolly Tree was an illustrator, part-time actress and costume designer, who came to real prominence in the 1930s. In the 1920s she was associated with Cabaret shows in particular and was engaged by the Café de Paris at the time of this novella to make and create all of the costumes for their Cabaret shows. Later her work became popular in Paris where she became the first English person to design for the Music Hall, the *Folies Bergère*.

9. The Lord Mayor of London, Sir Alfred Bower (1858–1948)

Sir Alfred Bower was a British businessman, specifically dealing as a wine merchant, elected as Sheriff of London in 1913 and knighted in the same year. He became Mayor of London in 1924, for the usual period of one year.

10. For Liberty, London, see:
https://www.libertylondon.com/

11. For the Café de Paris as it is today, see:
https://www.cafedeparis.com/

Thank you for joining Posie Parker

Enjoyed *Murder in the London Lights* (A Posie Parker Mystery #10)? Here's what you can do next.

If you could take a moment to leave a short review on the platform where you purchased the book, it would be immensely helpful.

Your reviews play a significant role in spreading the word about the series and assisting new readers in discovering it.

In addition to "Murder in the London Lights", Posie's other intriguing cases are available in various formats to suit your preference. You can find all the books, listed in chronological order here: https://www.amazon.com/author/lbhathaway

They are available in e-book and paperback formats, as well as in Audiobook format for those who prefer to listen.

Don't miss out! Take a moment to follow on Amazon and/or subscribe to the newsletter:

1. **Follow on Amazon:** Visit www.amazon.com/author/lbhathaway and click on "+Follow" button.

2. **Subscribe to the Newsletter:** Simply visit www.lbhathaway.com and enter your email address in the subscription box. By subscribing, you'll receive exclusive content, behind-the-scenes insights, and special offers straight to your inbox.

About the Author

Cambridge-educated, British-born L.B. Hathaway writes historical fiction. She worked as a lawyer at Lincoln's Inn in London for almost a decade before becoming a full-time writer. She is a lifelong fan of detective novels set in the Golden Age of Crime, and is an ardent Agatha Christie devotee.

Her other interests, in no particular order, are: very fast downhill skiing, theatre-going, drinking strong tea, Tudor history, exploring castles and generally trying to cram as much into life as possible.

The Posie Parker series of cosy crime novels span the 1920s. They each combine a core central mystery, an exploration of the reckless glamour of the age and a feisty protagonist who you would love to have as your best friend.

Get in touch with L.B. Hathaway or follow her on social media:

author@lbhathaway.com

Newsletter sign up:
https://www.lbhathaway.com

Goodreads:
https://www.goodreads.com/lbhathaway

Twitter:
https://twitter.com/LbHathaway

Facebook:
https://m.facebook.com/L-B-Hathaway-books-1423516601228019/

Made in United States
Troutdale, OR
09/25/2024